From award-winning author Jea
Global Ebook Award for Histori
twice finalist in the Wishing Sl
Society Editor's Choice, and fir.
Left Out, Book 1 of the series *L*
listed for the Cinnamon

PRAISE

"As a parent and a teacher, I felt this book in my gut. It hits so close to home on more levels than I can count. I felt for all those kids, all those teachers and parents trying, failing and succeeding at doing the best they can."
ANITA KOVACEVIC, TEACHER AND CHILDREN'S AUTHOR, CONTRIBUTOR TO THE INTERNATIONAL INNER GIANT ANTI-BULLYING PROJECT.

"A compelling story about friendship, its strength, and the unusual ways it develops."
REBECCA P. MCCRAY, *THE JOURNEY OF THE MARKED*

"A must for all left handers." AGL REVIEW

"Jean Gill brings her magical storytelling skills to teens, to weave compelling and thought-provoking stories that will linger on in their minds well after the last page is read."
KRISTIN GLEESON, AUTHOR AND CHILDREN'S LIBRARIAN

"I would most definitely recommend this book to a friend because it is very interesting."
SHAELAN SCOTT, TEEN TURF REVIEWER FOR *READERS REVIEW ROOM*

"This book was a short interesting read. It really moved me with how people will do every little thing they can to make what they believe get across to others."
CHARITY MARTINEZ, TEEN REVIEWER FOR 5 *GIRLS BOOK REVIEWS*

BOOKS BY JEAN GILL

Looking for Normal (teen fiction/fact)
Book 1 Left Out *(The 13th Sign)* 2017
Book 2 Fortune Kookie *(The 13th Sign)* 2017

Novels
Someone to Look Up To: a dog's search for love and understanding
(The 13th Sign) 2016

The Troubadours Quartet
Book 3 Plaint for Provence *(The 13th Sign)* 2015
Book 2 Bladesong *(The 13th Sign)* 2015
Book 1 Song at Dawn *(The 13th Sign)* 2015

Love Heals
Book 2 More Than One Kind *(The 13th Sign)*2016
Book 1 No Bed of Roses *(The 13th Sign)* 2016

Non-fiction/Memoir/Travel
How Blue is my Valley *(The 13th Sign)* 2016
A Small Cheese in Provence *(The 13th Sign)* 2016
Faithful through Hard Times *(lulu)* 2008
4.5 Years – war memoir by David Taylor *(lulu)* 2008

Short Stories and Poetry
One Sixth of a Gill *(The 13th Sign)* 2014
From Bed-time On *(National Poetry Foundation)* 1996
With Double Blade *(National Poetry Foundation)* 1988

Translation (from French)
The Last Love of Edith Piaf – Christie Laume *(Archipel)* 2014
A Pup in Your Life – Michel Hasbrouck *(Souvenir Press)* 2008
Gentle Dog Training – Michel Hasbrouck *(Souvenir Press)* 2008

First published in 2005 as *On The Other Hand* by y Lolfa
Cover and interior design by Jessica Bell
Cover and interior images © moypapaboris, Lubenica, frnsys, GooseFrol,
Anastacia - azzzya, Macrovector

LEFT OUT

JEAN GILL

FOR LESLEY, KERRY AND MY LEFT-HAND MAN.

Talent and all that for the most part is nothing but hogwash. Any schoolboy with a little aptitude might very well draw better than I perhaps; but what he most often lacks is the tough yearning for realisation, the teeth-grinding obstinacy and saying: even though I know I'm not capable of it, I'm still going to do it.

M.C. ESCHER, FROM A LETTER TO HIS SON ARTHUR 12TH FEBRUARY 1955

CHAPTER 1

"One-handed catch." Mrs Jones twirled round and threw the ball. "Jamie."

Jamie Williams fumbled the catch and dropped the ball. She picked it up slowly, her curly black hair covering her embarrassment. It wasn't as if this was new to her.

"Talk about the left hand not knowing what the right hand is doing," sniggered Kelly.

"Practice makes perfect," Mrs Jones reassured.

"Emma," muttered Jamie, and threw the ball across the circle with just enough venom to make it difficult, and not quite enough to get into trouble. Emma anticipated the flight, stepped backwards, jumped and caught the ball as if she were holding the Olympic flame in triumph.

"Well done, Emma. Did you see, Jamie, how Emma let her instincts take over so she could be in the right place, time it right, and let the hand-eye co-ordination take over. Practice, that's all it takes."

"Julie," signalled Emma, and the game continued.

As Jamie opened out her sweatshirt in the changing-room, her purse dropped out of its hiding place up her sleeve and rolled along the floor. She dived for it but too late to escape notice.

"Butterfingers," sang out Kelly, knotting her sweatshirt round her waist, where it dangled way below her school skirt. "Come on Donna – you're all fingers and thumbs today – it must be catching."

Again, Jamie let her hair hide her feelings, not helped by the fact that her shoe-lace had come undone. Like a bloody five-year-old, she thought gloomily, tying a double knot as Kelly walked off, arm in arm with Donna.

Outside the sports hall, Ryan was waiting for her. "Don't tell me, I can see by your face. We're going to be late for Science – we'd better hurry."

"I don't care. They're all so stupid. I think it's 'cos I'm left-handed that I drop things and feel a fool."

Ryan took her arm and steered her round along the corridor. "Or you say 'left' and mean 'right', or you turn the wrong way, or you fold the paper back to front. I know. How long have we been friends?"

"You're weird."

"Must be. Put a sorry face on, quick." As he walked into the classroom, he smiled ruefully at their Science teacher. "Sorry we're late Miss, Mr Harrison asked us to take a message."

As their group considered how to improve an electric circuit, Ryan mentioned casually, "Napoleon was left-handed. Didn't do him any harm."

Jamie shot a warning look at Jo and David, saying pointedly, "Why don't we put these batteries in the other way around." Some things were private.

"Eureka!" Jo pointed at the second bulb, which had lit up.

"That was bath water," Ryan told Jamie.

"What?" asked David. "I think the bulb's working. Did we use water?"

They all looked at him in exasperation.

"Never mind," Jamie said.

As they walked home through the back streets of Port Talbot, Jamie asked," How did you know?"

"How did I know what?"

"About Napoleon being left-handed."

"It's called research."

"Well, stop it. I don't like being a research project."

"Find out yourself, then."

"It's not like I'm disabled or something."

"What does that mean anyway, 'disabled'?"

"It means something's wrong with you."

"Well you do keep talking about being left-handed like there's something wrong with you."

"But that's more like, normal-something-wrong, just sort of different."

"So maybe that's what disabled is to whoever's disabled – it's normal-different."

"No." Jamie thought and shook her head again. "No." Another pause for thought. "And don't you call me disabled. I don't like it. Nerd."

"How about 'something challenged'? Like the way people say 'vertically challenged' instead of 'short', to be polite? We could call you 'co-ordination challenged'."

"Yeah, really slips off the tongue."

"I know, 'manually challenged'."

"Get a life. Yeah, that's you, life-challenged, socially challenged – you've got no friends and no one likes you."

"You're breaking my heart," responded Ryan cheerfully. It wasn't as if he didn't understand insults. Sometimes he even considered them, briefly. Then he shook his shaggy head and continued to think. Thinking was his hobby, and had left a few would-be-tormenters confused by him being so interested in them.

Their conversation paused automatically as they walked underneath the motorway flyover, without either of them noticing the traffic roar and the dull echoes against the concrete. At the junction they halted, before Ryan turned right, to the house up the hill where he lived with his mother, and Jamie turned left.

"I bet there's loads of famous people are left-handed – you

could try a search online," was Ryan's parting suggestion.

"Get a life!"

"Bet I can find hundreds..."

Jamie walked past one row of terraced houses, turned into an alley, unlatched the fourth gate along, slipped into the backyard, and then into the back porch and kitchen of her home. The good news was that her mother was home; the bad news was that so was her brother. The unmistakable sounds of her brother on vocals, and one of his friends murdering a drum kit, assaulted her ears as she passed the outbuilding still known as the coal shed, although it was years since it saw any black diamonds.

Jamie slung her bag onto a worktop in the kitchen where her mother was opening a can of beans. "How do you stick it, Mum! Can't they go somewhere else?"

"Don't leave your bag there – take it upstairs. And your brother says he's going to make a fortune with his band, so I'm not going to stand in his way. He tells me it's good to be Welsh and a pop star... like those super furry manics. Go and change out of your uniform and then I'll show you what's for tea."

"First glimpse of his chest they'd be reaching for the sickie bags. You working tonight?"

"You know I am – I told you what shifts I'm on." Jamie's mother worked around the corner at the supermarket. It proudly advertised its 24 hours opening and, as far as Jamie could work out, that's what her mother worked – 24 hours a day. No way was she going to be like that: she was going to get good qualifications, get a great job, be rich and never have children or do housework for anyone.

"I forget."

"You'd forget your head if it wasn't screwed on."

"That's 'cos I'm left-handed."

"No, it isn't, it's because you don't listen."

Jamie stomped upstairs with her bag, trying to shut out the attempts at harmony quavering from the coal shed. "I might only be in schoo-ul but I'd buy you lots of jew-uls – if I could." Her bedroom looked out onto the yard and a flash of colour attracted her attention.

Some girl was waggling across the yard in stacked heels, which pointed up towards a leather jacket above an inch of a red skirt. The familiar, pale, cat-face of Kelly Griffiths glanced up at the window, caught her watching, and smirked.

Kelly pretended to drop her purse, mimed being upset, threw the purse high in the air like a cheerleader, span round and caught it. With a little flip-kick, she disappeared into the coal shed. What was that little animal up to? Jamie slammed the window down on her brother's lyrics. In vain.

"We could hang around for hou-urs and I'd buy you lots of flow-ers – if I could." Three voices blended in the "If I could", before Jamie stuffed cotton wool in her ears.

Harmonies? Don't make her laugh. They would be hanging around for hou-urs singing about the flow-ers, she thought gloomily, as she dutifully went downstairs to get instructions for making tea for herself, Gareth and her Dad, who would be home from the steelworks.

How Jamie was supposed to remember who was working when, she had no idea, what with both parents on shifts. Dad on days and Mum on nights was supposed to be good for looking after her and Gareth – Jamie had heard them telling people that – but to Jamie it felt like living in a bus station where buses came and went all the time, and you just caught one when you could. She'd tried explaining it to Ryan but she could tell he just thought she was lucky having a brother and two parents, and so much going on.

"Take the cotton wool out of your ears," her mother was mouthing at her.

"What? I can't hear you." Jamie grinned when her mother gave her a play-clout. As she looked at a saucepan full of some brownish muck, Jamie was calculating her chance of a long session online. With her mother at work, her brother wowling in the coal shed with his friends, and her father not due home for two hours, she could get an hour without anyone knowing, and then she would claim she had home-work to do on the computer so she could carry on after tea.

The computer was in Gareth's bedroom, and, as he was older, their parents always gave him first shot at using it, for his homework. As if! Jamie had seen him up to some of his 'homework' but hers were typical parents – too stupid to know the difference between Science homework and him downloading song lyrics from a webzine. Ryan had made her curious, and she wondered if there really was any stuff out there about being left-handed.

"You might as well keep the cotton wool in!" Her mother was looking at her strangely and Jamie realised that she had taken sticks of dried spaghetti out of the packet, carefully putting one on top of the other to make a pile, and was now trying to remove a stick without bringing the pile down. She scooped all the spaghetti up, and crammed it back into the plastic bag, which tore and broke open, spilling its contents onto the floor.

"You're so clumsy!" Jamie's Mum was looking at her watch, flustered.

Jamie crimsoned. Seemed to be the word for the day, didn't it.

She would start a list of great people who were left-handed and the first name would be Jamie Williams, the second would be Napoleon, the third would be…Who would the third be? She had no idea whether there was anyone left-handed – apart from Napoleon, and, of course, herself in the future – who had ever done anything in the world. The sooner she got rid of her mother, the sooner she could get online.

"I'll do it. I'm fine. You get off to work." Jamie gave what she hoped was a reassuringly mature smile. It did the job and her mother left for work.

Jamie quickly checked through what she'd have to cook. Thank goodness it was pasta for tea. Jamie's left hand had many enemies and, along with scissors and can openers, she hated the potato peeler. All of them were created for right-handers, and had the cutting edge in the wrong place for Jamie. Having experimented with holding the potato peeler upside down, and using it with her right hand, which could never quite grasp the angle, she had given up. She always used a knife, which was less sensitive about angle, but which she also had to use with her right hand and which carved great chunks off the potato, earning her another telling-off if her mother saw her.

She took the stairs two at a time, barged into Gareth's bedroom, flung his school trousers, sweatshirt and last week's underpants off the chair onto the unmade bed, and switched on the computer. Angrily, she rearranged the desk so that the mouse was moved to the left side of the keyboard.

In reality, she was probably better at using the mouse with her right hand because she couldn't usually be bothered changing it over, especially in school, so she had hardly ever clicked left-handed. Today, however, she wanted to make a point.

'Left-handed people,' she keyed into the open search box and then as an afterthought added 'important', thought again and added 'intelligent good-looking world leaders'.

"Fetch!" she told the computer as she hit *Return*.

CHAPTER 2

Ryan was less pleased to find his mother at home but it was no surprise to him. She was a political journalist so worked from home, spending much of her time writing. They had moved to Port Talbot from London, England, chasing his mother's dream of the big story and limited by their funds as to where they could live.

Before London, and when he was too young to remember, it had been Montgomery, Alabama, where Ryan was born. His mother's precise English still held traces of a southern states' drawl. After she called Jamie "you all", his friend delighted in trying out the phrase for weeks, entertaining Ryan with a broad Port Talbot "yo-ew-orll" version of his mother's relaxed "y'all".

He had tried to explain to Jamie what was wrong with his mother but, "She's just too much" had been the best he could manage. She had opinions on everything. She would ask, "What do you think?" and then she would interrupt him, to ensure he reached the right conclusion and agreed with her.

He was the result of her opinions on bringing up children. Worse than that, he was the result of her opinions on the right of a single woman to be a mother. He couldn't remember a time when he didn't know he'd been fathered by a sperm bank, although he could remember thinking it was like the bank they went to for money, only you got babies there.

It had come as a shock to find out that other children had not been got from the bank, and he'd been lucky to move school again after *that* conversation. It wasn't that he blamed his mother exactly; there were just some things he'd rather not know or talk about.

Discussing everything was another of his mother's more difficult habits, and he deeply envied the way Jamie could hide within her own home, as people came and went all round her. He felt the pressure of his mother's attention like a TV camera and hand-held mike following him round, while a spotlight tracked him.

"Hi, hon, had a good day? Learn much?"

Mothers! "Good, fine, yeah."

"I thought I'd do Kentucky Fried Chicken tonight. Would you like that?"

"That would be great." His mother hated cooking and K.F.C. was treat food. What was she up to? "I'll go do some schoolwork." He escaped to his computer.

Perhaps he'd mail Jamie or even see if she was online in the chat room? No, he'd dig up some stuff on left-handers first. It would be good for his friend to have some role models.

His mother knew all the theory about role models and had bored him silly with details of sensitive, male, high achievers "just like he was going to be".

"One father would have been enough!" he'd shouted at her, one really bad time. That had led to several weeks of jolly men friends of his mother's visiting and having man-to-man chats with him, or talking about football, in which he had no interest.

He logged on, searched for 'famous left-handers', visited a couple of websites, and printed out some lists. He put circles around the interesting names, a few of which should leave Jamie well impressed. He went back over the names he'd circled, putting five stars by the best, until he'd got the names down to a top 10. He wanted a range of different types of famous people, and he had to make some tough choices.

In the end, it came down to Bill Clinton or Jimi Hendrix, and if you had to choose between a President of the United States and a tragic rock star who set the world and his guitar on fire, there was really no contest. He supposed he should have included some of the sporting heroes like Babe Ruth, only Jamie wouldn't have heard of the baseball player, or perhaps Jimmy Connors, but he thought tennis was boring. He made his choices and typed it up as a list to send to Jamie.

RYAN'S TOP 10 FAMOUS LEFT-HANDERS

ALBERT EINSTEIN: scientific genius who gave us the answer e=mc2. Before then, nobody knew there was a question.

NAPOLEON BONAPARTE: short Emperor of France who told his model-type tall girlfriend (another left-hander) "Not tonight Josephine". She must have told her friends, because he then lost a few wars, and was probably poisoned by arsenic in the green wallpaper on his prison island.

LUDWIG VAN BEETHOVEN: deaf composer of classical music who poured iced water over his head to help him think. Pity he and Hendrix didn't get together.

MICHELANGELO AND DAVID: Italian sculptor (Michelangelo) who took a second-hand piece of marble that some right-hander had chipped and turned it into the most famous statue in Europe: a left-handed giant-killer (David).

JIMI HENDRIX: tragic rock and roll star who set the world and his guitar on fire. Showed true left-handed versatility by not only re-stringing a right-handed guitar so he could play it but also by demonstrating how many parts of the body could play guitar if given the chance.

BILL GATES: millionaire with chips (silicone that is.)

LEONARDO DA VINCI: showed that writing notes backwards was actually a sign of genius, invented machines he could not have imagined and painted woman with strange smile and nagging tendencies (The Moaner, Lisa).

BART SIMPSON: anarchic under-achieving cartoon boy (Bart) and Max Groening: high-achieving cartoonist (Groening).

PRINCE CHARLES: God save him (and Camilla).

EMINEM: white rapper whose lyrics are more popular with his fans than with his wife, his mother or the police.

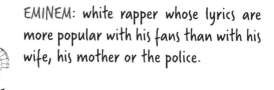

It had only taken him thirty minutes and now, perhaps, he would do some homework. He clicked *Send* and the email vanished into virtuality.

"…so I've been asked to take the piece to the States for a while, and it's such a great chance for you to get in touch with your roots. It's where we're from, Ryan and you'll love Atlanta; so much life and variety. We'll have time just to hang out together and you get to meet a whole new bunch of kids and salute the flag, sing *America the beautiful*, make up your own mind about the way the politicians there create national identity; such an opportunity."

Ryan's chicken was sticking in his throat. He had been through this before, only two years earlier, when they had moved from London so that his mother could attach herself to events at the Welsh Assembly and 'the emerging federal system in Britain', which meant the way Britain was becoming more like the USA, with the separate states of England, Wales, Scotland and Northern Ireland. Her dream was to get all her articles published as one book, *The United States of Britain*, and to make a fortune.

"How long is a while?" he asked quietly.

"It all depends. I need to get some American perspective,

interview some folks, make some contacts. A few months, maybe a year. Hey, I guess if y'all feel right at home, we could stay longer."

"What about school?"

"Don't you worry. They've got schools in the States all right; be a real experience for you."

"I'm having a real experience here."

"Don't you go sulk on me, now. You know I have to go where the work is. No work, no pay; no pay, no Kentucky fried. I know it's a change for you but you'll love it, you'll see."

"And we'll be coming back here?"

"Let's wait and see, shall we."

Ryan put the half-eaten drumstick down on the plate amid the cooling chips and stood up to leave the table.

"You haven't eaten your meal."

"I'm not hungry."

"Ry?" He ignored her and went upstairs to his room, shifting Hendrix to the top of his list for having publicly burnt the American flag.

Two hours of surfing, with a break for a rushed meal, left Jamie cursing the computer but finally grasping a list of left-handers' names. Her first search turned up some sites which would have made a teacher blush, the safest of which was a computer-dating agency. She clicked without thinking on one site name, blinked rapidly, told the screen image, "Put 'em away, love, for God's sake," and moved on.

After that, she deleted the word 'good-looking' from the search but still collected thousands of sites that seemed to have been selected at random, with no relationship to her search. She deleted words and tried again until she just searched for 'left-handed' and was a little more successful, although she still had a collection of odd information on supernatural powers and mystic healing mixed in with some more useful facts about being left-handed.

She sighed. What a waste of time. Ryan had encouraged her to use the internet, telling her "the Truth was out there". So were dustbinfuls of rubbish. She was about to log off and browse the lists, which she had printed, when an email arrived.

"Thanks a lot!" she told the cheerful message from Ryan. "Great timing." She printed off his list but doggedly read the fruits of her own research before she looked at his.

When she read his Top 10, she was angry enough to sit down and work out her own. Luckily, Gareth had gone off with his friends so she was free to write.

JAMIE'S TOP 10 LEFT-HANDERS

QUEEN VICTORIA: a working mother who ruled Britain when it was Great, had 11 children and was a legendary diary writer before Adrian Mole or Bridget Jones.

QUEEN ELIZABETH II: ditto, with diminished Greatness, fewer children and no diary.

CELINE DION: romantic Canadian singer who topped the charts with albums in both French and English and whose heart goes on... and on, when the Titanic goes down.

WHOOPI GOLDBERG: actress who is known for how good she is at acting: wish there were more like that.

PAULA RADCLIFFE: thinks a fun run is 22 miles in world record-breaking time.

MARTINA NAVRATILOVA: destroyed tennis opponents whichever hand she held her racket in: ambidextrous in her love life as well as her handedness.

MARIE CURIE: discovered radium when women were only supposed to discover new hair ribbons. She had to pretend her husband had carried out her research to get it taken seriously but she was too good to stay in the background for long.

JEANNE D'ARC: led the French armies to victory over the English: would she like to coach the Welsh rugby team?: and was burnt alive afterwards for being full of herself and wearing trousers.

JENNIFER SAUNDERS: absolutely fabulous comedian who proved that women could be funny. Why did women have to prove we could be funny? And who exactly did we have to prove ourselves to?

LEWIS CARROLL: brilliant Mathematician who wrote THE books for left-handers Alice in Wonderland and Alice through the Looking Glass for a little girl he knew (don't think too much about that). Used all his left-handed way of seeing the world to make puzzles. So successful in challenging reality that hip people in the swinging sixties thought Alice was on drugs.

Jamie added a PS to her email.

```
There is one man on my list because I'm not
being sexist - at least that's what some
people seem to think when there's one woman.
```

She banged down the key to send the message and shut down the system.

CHAPTER 3

"I'm sorry," Ryan hissed. "I didn't even notice they were all men, I just chose the ones who looked the most interesting."

"And you think that makes it better!" Jamie was outraged.

Ryan realised what he had said. "I'm making it worse, aren't I?"

"Keep digging, boy. Just don't expect a hand out of that hole."

"Why don't we make a new list together. We could write it up for the school magazine."

Their whispers had become too noticeable for the teacher trying to improve their Citizenship.

"Ryan, perhaps you could tell the class what the topic for the lesson is?" she challenged.

"Equal opportunities, Miss."

Jamie shook her head in admiration. He could always do that. She didn't know why the teachers bothered trying to catch him out.

"That's right, but I would appreciate a little more concentration on the lesson. Jamie, give some examples where people are not being given equal opportunities."

Jamie's brain did that teacher-question-uh-oh-blank-thing that it often did. There was one of *those* silences. "Can't think."

She heard Kelly mutter, "Say that again," loud enough to be heard but not loud enough to attract a reprimand.

"I can give an example," Ryan interrupted, and didn't wait for permission to carry on. "Everything's designed for right-handers, but loads of people are left-handed – really interesting, famous people."

"Like who?" someone demanded.

"Freddy Mercury," Ryan suggested.

"He was gay, he doesn't count." Donna dismissed the singer.

"Nicole Kidman."

"That's more like it – she's smart."

"Paul McCartney, Marilyn Monroe, Brad Pitt – there's loads of them."

"Don't forget your girlfriend." Kelly shared a smile with Donna.

"Read next week's *Afan Times*, you'll see an article by me and Jamie with our Top 10 famous left-handers and you'll be really surprised."

"Ryan!" Jamie tried to shut him up without looking once through the curly mop of hair she had allowed to fall forward over her embarrassment.

Mrs Davies had really had enough now. "You might be right, Ryan, about some difficulties for left-handers but that's off the point. As we've already said in the lesson, equal opportunities legislation is aimed at preventing discrimination on grounds of race, sex and disability – the main problems. I'd have thought you'd have been a bit more aware of that, Ryan," she looked meaningfully at him, "rather than throwing in red herrings."

Ryan had been frowning from the first few words she'd spoken and, unrepentant, he continued with his own line of thought, "You said I was 'right', Miss; that's prejudiced language – prejudiced against left-handers."

"Really, Ryan! For an intelligent boy, you can be so awkward. That's a different meaning of the word 'right' – you know it means 'correct'." She turned her attention firmly to the rest of the class. "Can someone give me a *good* example of prejudiced language?" She saw some of the dangers of the question and added quickly. "Politely, of course. Yes, Kelly?"

"Frogs, Miss, French people."

"Very good Kelly, now turn to Page 26 and we'll read about the reasons people leave their own countries and come to live in Wales."

Jamie was so angry she had forgotten she was not on speaking terms with Ryan. She felt like one of those weird, tropical, not-at-all French frogs with long tongues, as if she'd puff up all red until she exploded and spat poison at Mrs Davies. Luckily, she was left in peace for the rest of the lesson and, by lunch-time, her desire to sentence the offender to lengthy, gruesome torture (like in the 'crime and punishment' section of History lessons) had been reduced to the suggestion that they really ought to tell their Form Tutor.

"I mean, ask yourself, Ry, why did she say that about you, that you should know what's the important issues?"

Ryan shrugged. "Maybe she thinks I'm gay. She didn't like to say that as a prejudice did she." He laughed.

"Don't be daft. We both know why she said it to you. That's what I mean, she shouldn't be doing it, picking on you like that."

"She's wrong."

"That's what I'm telling you."

"No, not about that, forget it, doesn't matter. No, I mean about prejudice against left-handers – it does matter."

Jamie hung her head. "I don't want you making a fuss, Ry. It's just embarrassing"

"This isn't about you." He had that light in his eyes. "It's about ten percent of the human race."

"Well, yeah, but it's about me too."

"This is your chance to stand up and speak up. Let's go see Mr Travis so we can run something in the magazine, like I said we would."

"But Ry–"

"Come on."

"Has anyone ever told you how like your mother you are?"

"Don't go there."

Mr Travis was bearded and fierce, with a sense of humour that left his classes uncertain whether to laugh or dive for cover. He was however so enthusiastic about English that, according to rumour, boys would send their sisters to the library to borrow books that he had recommended.

Jamie had probably started the rumour after Gareth had asked her to get *Holes* for him to read. For weeks, he was coming out with comments, at home, like 'I can't believe they had to dig holes in the desert' and 'The way you see those red nails... and it's snake venom'.

Mr Travis also produced a school magazine and a weekly column for the local newspaper. Sometimes Ryan would write a piece, sometimes he would avoid Mr Travis for weeks, but, most importantly, his mother was not to know. This was understood by Travis and, of course, Jamie, and Ryan wrote under the pseudonym of *Myrddyn*, the Welsh for Merlin, so his published articles would not give him away. Of course, the other kids knew who Myrddyn was but Ryan thought it highly unlikely that his mother would have a good old chat with his classmates, so his secret was safe.

Jamie found his choice of pseudonym weird; "I mean, it's a bit Welsh for you."

Ryan had merely replied, "I used it for the Eisteddfod, when we were all told to choose Welshy names, and it brought me luck. Besides, for all I know it could be my Celtic ancestry – on my father's side."

The moment he decided she was enough of a friend to take home, Ryan confided all his family background in Jamie. He knew full well that if he didn't, it would only be minutes before his mother did.

"Don't think so, boy." They both laughed. Jamie told him that his mother would be dead chuffed if she knew he was turning into a journalist, and he gave her one of those withering looks, and said that was why she must never know. Jamie would never understand the mother/son thing, and it wasn't like that with Gareth and their own Mum. Ryan was so complicated.

"Great idea," was Mr Travis' response, as he drew red lines across an exercise book and wrote 'You must improve your handwriting' in that tiny, slanting scrawl which no one could read. "So, you're going to write about sporting heroes."

"No," Ryan sighed, and explained again.

Mr Travis beamed. "So, there will be some sporting heroes! That's great. We're trying to make more effort to interest boys, you see."

"I'm a boy!" Ryan said, insulted.

"So am I actually," confided Mr Travis, "and I love the

stuff you write. What's more," he fixed Jamie with one of his looks, "I love the stuff you write too. In fact, I'd like more from you, whether it's with Ryan or not." Jamie felt as if someone had thumped her in the chest with a bunch of flowers, the sort of present that winded her.

"How many column inches, Sir?"

Mr Travis waved his red pen in the air. "I'm not what you might call overwhelmed with column inches, so the more, the better. Just write something good."

They turned to go and the teacher's head was already bent back over his marking when he called after them, "Oh, and Ryan? Jamie? If you could include a sporting hero or two?"

"Sir."

When she arrived home from school, Jamie was disappointed to find Gareth occupying his own bedroom. She had hoped that she would be able to use the computer, to find out more for their article.

"You gonna be long?"

"Going out after tea."

"Spares us the row then, dunnit."

Gareth gave a big mock-sigh without taking his attention off the joystick and the multi-coloured explosions on the screen. "That's you off my list for getting money when I'm rich and famous. Yes! He shoots, he scores!" The screen flashed up a score and a message of congratulations which

Gareth barely paused to read before clicking *Yes* to *Want to play again?*.

"In your dreams," muttered Jamie. "What was Kelly Griffiths doing here?"

"Why? Friend of yours?"

"Just someone in my class."

"Just hanging out with the band. She's all right – for a kid."

Jamie's relief when she finally sat down at the computer and searched for 'left-handed' turned to growing anger – and this time it wasn't at Ryan but at what she discovered.

Ryan had volunteered to turn their joint research on famous left-handers into the first article, promising Jamie that he

Question: What do the following people have in common, apart from being famous?

would combine their lists and see if he could add one or two more sporting heroes to keep everyone happy.

He was experimenting with openings. He thought he would go for a rhetorical question:

Then came the list that he and Jamie had drawn up, to which he added,

Monica Seles, Pablo Picasso, Judy Garland, Isaac Newton, Lord Nelson, Bruce Willis

Answer: They were all left-handed

or

Question: Who was the greatest footballer who ever lived, scoring 1,282 goals in 1364 games and helping Brazil win the World Cup three times?

Answer: Edson Arantes do Nascimnento, better known as Pele.

Then he could drop in the idea that Pele was left-handed and left-footed. If he could also get in the fact that Ryan Giggs was a left-footer, Mr Travis would be over the moon. Ryan frowned. He just hoped that it wouldn't put off everyone who thought there was more to life than eleven men chasing a ball, or even fifteen men chasing a ball. Writing for a particular audience was cramping his creative style. He stood up, paced about the room a bit, lay on the floor with his feet up against the wall and walked out a rhythm against it.

"Cut it out, Ry," came the predictable call from downstairs, "and make sure there's no marks on that wall." His mother's response sounded more routine than angry, which meant she was still being nice to him, which meant they were still moving.

Sometimes she'd threaten a move and it would fall through, or she'd change her mind. No such luck this time, so it seemed. He'd have to tell Jamie some time. He tapped out a last rap on the wall, then turned right way up, to inspect the damage. A neatly criss-crossed pattern of trainer tracks decorated the pale blue wall. Sneaker tracks, as his Mum would call them. Or something far worse. All his life Ryan had been told, "Don't leave any marks; it's not our house," and every now and again the urge to leave his mark was too strong.

He sighed and returned to the job of adding sports facts to his piece.

"Tabloid journalism," he muttered to himself, "selling out," but his quick fingers typed out,

a) Name 5 sports which favour a left-hander?

b) Which sport bans a left-hander?

c) Name a sport which makes left-handers and right-handers compete.

Ryan wondered if he should count 'astronaut' and 'pilot' as sportspeople but decided, the hell with it – he'd expand his readers' minds.

He turned up the radio, paused, then turned it up even more.

"Ryan, can you turn that thing down a bit?"

He grinned and ignored her. It was a sure way of finding out how quickly they'd be moving. If it was really soon, she'd bite her tongue and put up with him.

Ryan lost himself in his writing, and there were no further comments from his mother downstairs.

ANSWERS:

a) Judging by the high proportion of left-handers, it's good to be left-handed in tennis, swimming, flying to the moon, piloting a plane, baseball (sometimes not so much because of the left-handedness itself but because left-handers are more likely to be ambidextrous, or because there are fewer left-handers than right-handers).

Many sports-people in cricket, fencing and basketball say that being left-handed gives them the advantage of coming out with unexpected plays.

b) Polo, so left-handed Prince Charles has to play polo right-handed (Field hockey also bans left-handers).

c) Archery.

CHAPTER 4

Despite Ryan mailing her copies of his article and repeatedly asking to see what she had written, Jamie refused to show him her latest research.

"You'll see it when it's published," she told her friend and wrapped her arms around herself, bursting with secret knowledge.

When she had given her piece to Mr Travis, he had smiled his lopsided smile, telling her "Great stuff!" as he skimmed it and spoiling it by adding "Hope you used a spellcheck this time."

Ryan was inevitably a bit miffed at being left out – *'left' out, huh!* Jamie thought – but it was only for a few days and it would be worth it to see his reaction to reading something that *she* had written and which, she hoped, would actually be *news* to him. After all, she was the expert on being left-handed; this should be her campaign. She put Ryan out of her mind and went looking for her brother, to talk him into helping her with her plan.

Gareth's first reaction was "No way – it's a stupid idea. You're only going to wind up Mum and Dad, and as for school – can you imagine what the teachers are going to say!"

However, when she had explained to him that it was the

only way for people to understand what things had really been like for left-handers in the past, and especially when she mentioned the beer that he'd been sneaking into the coal shed, and how Mum and Dad would be too wound up when she mentioned *that* to them to even notice what she was up to, it was amazing how quickly he saw reason.

"Anyway, you're in college so no one will say anything to you about it, if you're too much of a wimp to join in," had been her clinching argument.

Jamie's Mum was home for tea all this week which meant that Jamie didn't have to cook, but which also meant that they sat at the table instead of sprawling in front of the television or – Jamie's preference – walking around and eating at the same time.

It was so boring to sit still and it was quite likely that someone would have a go at someone else when they were all together. When that happened, Jamie's throat would close like a trap so that she couldn't eat and then as soon as someone noticed, she'd get shouted at for not eating, which only made it worse.

Was she sure she wanted to do this? What had Ryan said? "This is your chance to stand up and speak up." She thought of all the unfairness of it and when her Mum called, "Food's on the table," she was ready.

"Now," she urged Gareth, passing him the string and

sitting down at the table.

"Not so tight, idiot!" she hissed.

"Thought you wanted it realistic," he grinned, inspecting the knot professionally. "Reef knot – you'll never get out of that."

"Thanks." Jamie's stomach churned. The clatter of dishes and whir of the cooker hood had covered their conversation, and her father, as always, was last to arrive for the meal, and to weary to notice anything other than whether the food was hot.

Once she had served up the pie and chips, her mother was sharper, and it only took a few splodges of pie dropped on the table before her mother said, "Jamie, what the hell's the matter with you? And why have you got one hand behind your back?"

Jamie swallowed. "I'm writing something for the school magazine about the way left-handers have been persecuted in history and–" her father's fork had stopped half-way up to his mouth, and she carried on in a rush before she lost her nerve. "And parents used to tie a child's left hand behind her back to make her right-handed and they thought that it was a sign of the devil and they did terrible stuff and I just wanted to see what it's like to not be able to use your left-hand for eating and it's horrible... not just the eating... you can't even put your hair out of your eyes with the proper hand and the string doesn't half rub–"

"That's enough!" Horrified, Jamie watched her father's fork slowly coming lower onto the plate, and her mother's hand moving to her father's forearm, to calm him. He shook off the hand and his wife's low appeal, "Mark..."

"I dunno what we send you to that school for, putting stupid ideas into your head."

"Told you," muttered Gareth, unwisely.

"And you're a fine example to your sister. God knows what you do in that college wasting our money and can't even do a proper course. Sports Science! Don't see a lot of jobs advertised for sports scientists round here! And the rest of the time making an unholy row in my shed. And as for you," her dad returned to Jamie, pointing at her. "Swear to God there's something wrong with you, girl. Anyone needs to go tying themselves to a chair to see what it's like's gorra few bricks missing. And I don't work my backside off all day to have to listen to your nonsense about how tough it is for left-handers when I come home. Try finding out how tough it is down the steelworks. Sooner she leaves school the better."

Jamie almost forgot her demonstration. "But I want to go to university."

"Well you find the trees, girl."

What trees?" Jamie asked, bemused.

"The trees the bloody money grows on." Her father stood

up. "I'm going out," he told the air, and they heard him grabbing a coat and then the slam of the front door.

"Oh, Jamie," reproached her mother.

"I don't care! I've got to stand up for what's important to me." She thought of Mrs Davics, her father, her mother, even Gareth. "You're all the same! It's only what you think is important that counts!" She twisted to flounce up to the room but merely burnt the string across her left arm.

"Gareth!" she demanded between gritted teeth, "Get it off!"

Gareth struggled with his knot, and it was her mother, with scissors from the kitchen drawer, who snipped through the offending string, and released Jamie. She managed to close the kitchen door behind her before she rubbed the raw, burnt skin on her arm, and let the tears come as she rushed up to the sanctuary of her bedroom.

Later, a gentle knock came on her door. "Jamie?"

"What?" she answered her brother ungraciously.

"Can I come in?" He didn't wait for an answer but came and sat on the end of her bed. She sniffed and rubbed at her eyes.

"I did tell you."

"I don't care."

"How did it feel?"

"Great. I love Dad shouting at me and telling me I can't go

to university."

"No, not that. The experiment. Not being able to use your left hand."

"Bad. Different kinds of bad." She thought back. "The obvious, like dropping stuff because I'm not used to using my right hand for some things anyway, and then you've only got one hand so you can't do two things at one. It's amazing how often you use both hands at the same time when you're eating. So it makes you clumsy."

"Clumsier" Gareth punched her lightly. "Only joking," he added anxiously. "So, what else?"

"Feelings. It's OK at first, you think I'm just trying this out to see what it's like, and then it gets more and more frustrating every time you try to use your left hand and you can't. It's like your body's crying, and it makes your brain feel tired from telling your body not to mind."

"Sounds schizo. Anyway, it was only for a few minutes, and you only had to ask."

"But that's not what it felt like. What must it have been like if it was against your will? From when you were really little? My arm hurts like hell – what if I'd been struggling and fighting it. Gareth, it was so cruel! What if people are still doing it?"

"No, that's old-days stuff, like sticking people in the stocks or stoning them."

"They still do that in some places."

"Dad was mental."

"Yes." They contemplated the implications gloomily.

"Why?" asked Jamie.

"Who knows.? Bad day at work, or doesn't like seeing young girls tied up." It was Jamie's turn to grin and punch her brother. "That's better. I don't know," he hesitated, "I mean, did you ever wonder where you got your left-handedness from?"

"Dunno if it's hereditary. Anyway, both Mum and Dad are right-handed. Unless you mean," she used a drama-queen soap opera voice, "he's not my father."

"Oh, he's our father all right. But maybe he didn't start off right-handed. Isn't that what your experiment was about."

Jamie thought. "He'd have said."

"Would he?" The question hung in the air.

"Are you still going ahead in school?"

"Yes." She was even more determined now, especially as the magazine would come out the next day, with her and Ryan's articles. "But I'm not using string again." She would show them all.

CHAPTER 5

STAND UP FOR YOUR LEFTS!

The English language is prejudiced against left-handers.

We are tired of being left out while you are in the right.

The word 'left' is from the Saxon word 'lyft', which had two meanings — 'left' and 'useless'.

IT IS NOT ALL LEFT TO MAKE SOMEONE ELSE FEEL INFERIOR — BAN THESE WORDS!

WORD	MEANING
maladroit	clumsy, from the French for bad on the right
gauche	clumsy, from the French for left
sinister	wicked, from the Latin for left
awkward/gawky	clumsy/uncoordinated, from the Middle English awke, meaning from the left
adroit	deft/clever with hands, from the French for right
dexterous	good with hands, from the Latin for right
ambidextrous	good with both hands, from the Latin for having two right hands
righteous/right	good, straight, correct, not left, from the Latin for straight, right (side)

To have two left feet = to be clumsy
IS IT ANY WONDER WE LEFT-HANDERS FEEL CLUMSY?!!

WHAT DID THE ROMANS EVER DO FOR US?

The Romans invented the right-handed handshake as a way of showing you were not carrying a weapon … but if you were left-handed, you could shake hands right-handed AND stab someone with the dagger in your left hand — SINISTER

The Romans gave us our alphabet which reads from left to right — Could that be why more left-handers are dyslexic?

?dednah-tfel uoy erA

?ylisae siht daer uoy naC

?ylisae erom siht daer uoy naC

.tfel-ot-thgir ni seiraid sih etorw icniV ad odranoeL

SO YOU THOUGHT THE ROMANS WERE PREJUDICED?

The Devil was left-handed —
and left-handers belonged to *The Devil*
according to superstition and medieval Christianity.
That's why you're supposed to throw spilt salt over your left
shoulder, which is where the Devil will be.

Being left-handed could be evidence to burn someone as a witch.

That's why Christian characters in religious paintings are supposed to be right-handed and the best place is 'seated on the right hand' (but left-handed artists risked death and painted it their own way) Leonardo da Vinci painted Jesus and Mary as left-handers Michelangelo even painted *GOD* as *left-handed* on the Sistene Chapel ceiling in Rome).

That's also why the Christian Church decreed that left-handed children should be forced to become right-handed, to rid them of the Devil.

UNBELIEVABLE CRUELTY IN THE 20TH CENTURY

Even in the 20th century children were forced to become right-handers by their parents and their schools. *Terrible things* were done to them. Their left hands were tied up and thwacked with rulers. Some children even had heavy weights attached to their left hands or were scalded with boiling water over their left hands if they tried to use them.

As a demonstration in memory of all those left-handers who have been *tortured* because of *ignorance* and *prejudice*, your *left-handed* Times Reporter, *Jamie Williams*, will spend one whole day in school with her left hand tied up.

Show your support with a left-handed salute!

Some people still think it is bad to be left-handed.

THEY ARE WRONG!!!
In our next edition;
Forget the Romans — what about the Incas, the Greeks, the Chinese and the Arabs?
Living in a right-handed world — and succeeding there!

Jamie watched Ryan's face carefully, but she couldn't hug herself because of the long scarf tying up her left arm in a sling arrangement. Gareth had been as good as his word, and it had been well worth keeping her secret, to see the gobsmacked expression on Ryan's face. They had come early to school, rushed straight to Mr Travis' classroom where they found him with what looked like the same pile of books.

"Do you think he sleeps here?"

He hadn't even looked up, just passed the two copies of the latest edition of *The Afan Times*, muttered "Well done," and put a big red tick in a book, so that they couldn't be sure whether he was talking to them or the anonymous pupil whose book he was marking.

They decided not to risk further interruption, and they found the quietest corner they could, sandwiched between the wooden coat-rails of a disused cloakroom, which dated from the days when presumably coats could be left there without being nicked. Jamie couldn't concentrate on Ryan's 'famous left-handers', which he'd seen before anyway, for glancing sideways to see what he thought of her article. She still couldn't believe she'd done it, let alone put her name up front for the world to see, declared in bold as a left-hander.

"Well?" she asked him. Ryan was speechless, just staring at her and making bubbling noises. He hadn't even noticed her arm, hidden as it was under her coat, again with help from her brother. Time for the coat to come off! She wriggled but it was too difficult.

"Help me with this, Ry!" Even with help to remove the coat, she still had the job of unzipping her bag, putting the coat in, and zipping the bag up again – one handed.

"You have no idea how difficult it is to undo a zip one-handed," she complained, "and the wrong hand, too."

It was going to be a very long day, almost as long as the day they'd done a sponsored silence – some teacher's bright idea that had been!

"You should have told me. I can join in. Tie me up too," Ryan demanded.

Jamie gave a helpless shrug. "I can't even open my bag, never mind tie you up."

"I'll get someone else to." He was already looking around for someone in their class. Jamie glowed with the knowledge that for once *he* was desperate to follow *her* lead but she also wanted to keep ahead this time.

"Ry, if we're both tied up, we'll both be helpless. I need you to do stuff, like open my bag."

He looked dejected, then brightened. "The salute! I can do the salute with you, so we get everyone joining in, like you said in the article. How does the salute go?"

"Like this." Jamie tried to move her left arm, remembered, and was mortified. "I can't believe it – I forgot! I can't do it."

Ryan brightened even more. "So, you do need me. Tell me how it goes."

"You know the way the sportsmen smack their right hand onto their heart when the national anthem's playing? Do it the other way round, left hand onto right chest. Snappier, more military. That's it."

The bell rang, and they waited the customary minute before sauntering along to registration, Ryan saluting bemused kids as the corridors surged with purposeful movement.

"Ow, watch yourself." Jamie found herself frequently bashed on her vulnerable left side. "You don't realise how useful your elbow is." Someone trying to overtake on her right was efficiently repelled by her bag, reinforced by her right elbow. "I hate carrying my bag on the right. Nothing's where it should be."

One or two of the younger kids had picked up Ryan's salute, and were mimicking him, sniggering. He gave them all the same bountiful smile as if they were puppies in need of encouragement.

"Little runts," was Jamie's view.

"You wait," Ryan responded between the ever-gleaming teeth, adding loudly to the corridor at large, "Read *The Afan Times*."

They could see copies of the magazine being dropped off at each classroom and Jamie felt her stomach fluttering.

Hundreds of people were going to see the words she had written. She went over every word in her mind, living it again in the mind of her readers.

"Look out, you wallie!" She turned so that she could use her right arm to clout a small boy who had tried to duck between her and the wall on her left. "You want to live, be patient."

Head down, he hardly paused but, like a clockwork toy banging into a piece of furniture, he merely re-routed himself to charge around another way.

"They get worse every year," muttered Ryan.

Although Jamie felt as conspicuous as a giant pimple, nobody seemed to notice her, or her tied arm, and she settled gratefully into the day's routine. She wasn't even sure that their Maths teacher noticed her struggling to write with her right hand, as the paper shifted about and she tried to hold it in place with her left elbow. At least it was mostly numbers, so she could just about read back what she had written. It was like looking over her books from infant school. Even Kelly's jibe at Ryan could not deflate Jamie's enthusiasm.

As Ryan cheerfully clapped his left hand on his chest to salute classmates, Kelly sneered, "We already know you're a right tit – no need to show us."

Second lesson was Citizenship and Mrs Davies was waiting in her doorway to usher them in. When she saw Jamie, her expression changed, showing an unexpected warmth. She even made the others give room for Jamie to come in without her arm being knocked.

"What did you do to your arm, Jamie?" she asked in a concerned, motherly tone.

Before Jamie could explain, Kelly spoke. "She hasn't done nothing. She's tied it up herself for a bit of attention."

Mrs Davies' face clouded over, reddening at being taken in.

"Miss, I—" Jamie began.

"Get that off your arm at once! And the rest of you hurry up and sit down."

Jamie sat down.

"Miss, Jamie's showing—" Ryan tried, but was cut off mid-word by an increasingly irritated Mrs Davies.

"Enough, Ryan. Jamie, I told you to take that off."

Jamie's mouth was a thin line of determination. She just hoped no one could hear her heart banging on her ribs. It was a matter of principle, she reminded herself, as she opened her textbook with her right hand. Think of all the persecution suffered by left-handers before her. This was the least she could do on their behalf. It was nothing.

Mrs Davies used her quiet-but-deadly voice. "You have thirty seconds to do as I have told you, Jamie, or I will have to refer you." Jamie had never been referred in all her time in school. She wasn't even sure what it meant. She swallowed and looked anywhere but at Mrs Davies, desperately avoiding her eyes.

"You leave me no option." The teacher wrote something on a piece of paper, gave it to Jamie, who clutched it in her only available hand. "Show that note to the secretary and wait outside the Office. If anyone asks you why you're there, tell them Mrs Davies sent you."

She was being sent to the Head! Jamie felt her chin and her knees wobble, and she just hoped it didn't show as she stood up. Could she get suspended just for this? The trouble with being a good girl, she thought bitterly was that you didn't know what happened to naughty girls. And then, if you accidentally became one, you didn't know what to expect.

"But Miss–" Ryan never knew when he was beaten.

She turned to glare at him. What use would he be if he got sent out with her. "Bring my bag, after," she muttered, hoping he would get the message. Whether he had or not, she couldn't tell, but Mrs Davies pretended not to hear him, and he let it pass.

"Right, everyone. Turn to Page 25." Dismissed, Jamie closed the classroom door behind her.

"Right," she told herself, wincing at the unfortunate choice of word, and she took her time to walk the length of the school and stand like a sentry outside the closed door of the

Head's Office.

"Bitch!" Ryan hissed at Kelly as Mrs Davies wrote on the whiteboard. As soon as the bell rang, he was down the corridor like Ashley Cole down the left wing, to beat Mrs Davies and be with Jamie when she gave her side of the story. He tried to think of anything he knew about the Head that would help, but the only time he had been in that Office had been with his mother when he first came to the school. Everyone had been so nice to each other it was sickening. It was hardly going to be like that now, was it. Like Jamie, he worried about her getting suspended. It didn't take a genius to imagine how her father would react.

He turned the corner, swinging both bags like a windmill, and stopped dead. Racing behind Ryan, Kelly stopped just short of him, saw what he saw, and vanished back into the corridor crowd. The Head's door was shut, there was no one standing outside; Jamie was not there.

CHAPTER 6

Jamie was standing outside the Head's Office, counting the spots of brown paint which had missed the wall and landed on the window, when the door beside her opened, and out came a man in a grey suit. Jamie straightened up, taking her back and foot away from the support of the wall, but not before she was seen by the Head and given an ominous glare.

"Looks like you have a young visitor," commented Mr Suit cheerfully.

"Probably a message." The Head glared at Jamie again behind Mr Suit's back. They walked away from Jamie towards the School Office and exit. "Business sponsorship would be useful to develop the canteen plans... perhaps we can mention it to Philip tonight? He's been so generous in the past."

"We'll ask the usual people, see if hands go into pockets, and what we manage without begging from the Authority..." The voices trailed off, and there was a silence, during which Jamie was looking for people's faces in the random lines patterning the floor. She thought she could see left-handers Marilyn Monroe and Oprah Winfrey, and if she squinted she could see Uri Geller in the act of bending spoons.

The returning footsteps were horribly purposeful and

followed by the expected "Come into my office," then, "Sit down."

Jamie sat. She held out the note Mrs Davies had written, which had somehow scrunched itself up, and waited.

Jamie looked nervously around the room while the Head scanned Mrs Davies' note. Art work and poems by pupils were on the walls, framed; there was a pair of black and white pictures, not by pupils – one showed white fish changing as a pattern so that they became black birds, and the other showed two hands, each one drawing the cuff of the other one so the image looked half-animated and half real; a noticeboard had school information documents tacked neatly to it. The window looked onto a tiny concrete courtyard which no one used, and where some daffodils were dying back to brown in a small tub.

Jamie checked her right wrist and sighed; according to her watch, the class was still only half-way through Citizenship, and there was no way Ryan could reach her before the end of the lesson. On the plus side, Mrs Davies couldn't reach her either.

Jamie's attention shifted to the desk, which was not as tidy as the rest of the room. There was a pile of documents in small print to the left of the Head, the top one skewed as if opened for reading, and a neat tray to the right with a few sheets in it, dated and ticked. A familiar name and font among the documents caught Jamie's eye, even though the text was upside down; she could see what Ryan insisted on calling 'the Banner' of *The Afan Times*.

"I need to speak to Mrs Davies," the Head warned, "but it seems you have pretended to hurt your arm to get out of writing in lessons, then been incredibly rude to Mrs Davies and defied her. What do you have to say for yourself, Jamie?"

Jamie wondered whether the Head was just repeating the name on the note or whether she really knew her, Jamie's name. The word was that the Head knew everyone, not just their names, but their grades, their report comments and their detentions – especially their detentions.

"I..." Jamie stuttered. She reached across the desk towards the Head's pile of documents.

"Don't touch those!"

Jamie jumped at the whip in the voice. Then she realised that it couldn't be any worse, so she had nothing to lose. Suddenly she could speak. "*The Afan Times*. If you look in that, it will explain."

The elegant arch to the Head's eyebrows said it all, but Jamie was allowed to pick up *The Afan Times* and point to the announcement of the proposed demonstration by 'your left-handed *Times* reporter, Jamie Williams'.

"And presumably you planned this 'demonstration' carefully, checked with your teachers, gained permission properly?"

Jamie was mortified. "I didn't think, Miss."

"No, you didn't," was the blunt reply.

The silence stretched into the destruction of all Jamie's hopes for the future, any future. The Head's fingers drummed lightly on the magazine.

"So, Mr Travis knew?"

"I suppose. I mean, he must have seen it when he published it." Jamie had a sudden image of him marking, talking and collecting articles, all at the same time. She rushed to defend him against the implied criticism. "But the file was ready, he didn't need to check it, he trusts us and he's so busy, he's working all the time, so he probably didn't read every word..." she tailed off, not sure whether she was making things better or worse. It was no good if the Head went easy on her, then took it out on Mr Travis.

"Us?" queried the Head. "That would be you and *Myrddin*?"

"Yes, me and Ryan. He thought we should stand up against prejudice, and he knows all about me being left-handed."

"Ryan? That is Ryan Anderson?"

"Yes."

"And Ryan thought it important to stand up against prejudice?"

"Yes, prejudice against left-handers."

"That's interesting, very interesting."

"And we were trying to talk about it in Citizenship, but

Mrs Davies only wanted to talk about what she wants to talk about, like she decides what's prejudice and what's important, and she even told Ryan that she thought he'd know better about what's important, and that cheesed off both of us and we're doing loads of research now, and Mr Travis says it's interesting."

She registered the shadow chasing across the Head's face. "I shouldn't have said that, about Mrs Davies. I... it wasn't really her fault this morning... she thought I was winding her up." Hardly surprising after Kelly's helpful little comment. She would deal with that herself, if she ever got out of this Office.

"All right Jamie. I get the picture." Jamie could tell that the judgement was made.

"We both know that you owe Mrs Davies an apology and that the misunderstanding – and I do think it is a misunderstanding – is entirely your fault." Jamie took the full weight of a steely look from those blue eyes. "You should have thought it out a bit more beforehand. But I think your heart is in the right place, and we owe it to our left-handed *Afan Times* reporter – and your readers – to let you finish your day of demonstration.

I'm writing you a note that I want you to show to your teachers – at the beginning of each lesson. It will explain what you're doing, and that you have my permission." The

Head was writing as she spoke and Jamie watched, fascinated, as the Head hooked up her arm in the habit characteristic of left-handers, so that they would be able to see what they were writing and not smudge it.

"You're left-handed," Jamie blurted out.

"Don't you just hate the way a ring-binder catches your writing-hand, and having to try can-openers and scissors and corkscrews with your right hand?" Was that a twinkle in the Head's eyes?

"And when you play cards – if you put the cards tidy, you can't see any of the numbers, and the fastener on a cycle helmet." Jamie shook her head.

"What is it like," the Head asked, "having your left hand tied up?"

"Awful." Jamie grinned, "but I reckon I'm better than Ry would be if his right hand was tied up. Us left-handers are more like ambi-thingie, because we have to be."

"Dextrous, ambidextrous." She pointed at the black and white pictures on the wall. "See the picture, *Drawing Hands*, there? One right hand, one left hand, challenging our perceptions. Left-handed artist, Escher, definitely one you should add to your list. No more demonstrations after today, OK?" Jamie nodded. "Break's nearly over. You'd better get off to third lesson."

"Can I interview you? For the magazine? As a famous left-hander?"

The Head had already returned to her documents and didn't look up. "Intrepid reporter, Jamie Williams. Tomorrow, one o'clock. Off you go."

It was a triumphant Jamie who returned to the Head's Office the next day, with Ryan. They were given half an hour to put their questions and it was just as well Ryan insisted on taping the interview, because Jamie couldn't write quickly enough to get the answers down. Even when they replayed the tape at Ryan's house, that night, they kept missing bits and having to rewind.

At first, they tried to write the whole interview out but when they realised how much writing thirty minutes' talk could turn into, and how many 'ums' and 'ers' and repetitions, they decided they would have to pick out the best bit. That meant a lot of shouting "Stop! Back a bit... there, there!"

Ryan's mother had called up, "What are you two up to?"

"Schoolwork," they had yelled down.

Finally, they were happy with what they had written. They would have to show the Head first before it went to Mr Travis, but they didn't think there would be any problems.

EXCLUSIVE!

AFAN TIMES REPORTERS, JAMIE WILLIAMS AND MYRDDIN INTERVIEW AFAN'S VERY OWN LEFT-HANDED SUPER-HEAD, MEGAN CARTER.

Could you tell us, Mrs Carter, when you first knew you were left-handed?

Well, it wasn't so much that I knew I was left-handed as that I suddenly realised other people were not. I must have been about six, I think.

Did your parents mind?

Both my parents were left-handed so it seemed normal — it was normal.

Do you have any brothers or sisters?

One of each and, before you ask, they're both right-handed, but that was fine too. We never thought about it.

Has anything been difficult for you because you're left-handed?

I know some left-handers find it difficult to read and write — but

then so do some right-handers. That was no problem for me. But there are lots of tools that are tricky — I have to use my electric drill right-handed, and the button for the electric saw is on the right side, the strimmer is right-handed... I needed to cut through some long grass with a scythe and you just can't use that left-handed.

You seem to use a lot of tools.

It's a good break from work to get outside, build something, repair something or do the gardening. We have a big garden... A bit of manual work is good for stress relief and to stop you thinking too much.

I do find it difficult to lay a table, but that's because I like my knife and fork set out left-handed, and then I'm not sure about where they go for other people. Clocks... sometimes I read the clock backwards... I prefer digital timepieces!

Another thing is that I can get confused about directions... if someone says "Turn right," then I can muddle left and right. I think that's because I have to do so much switching, sometimes having to turn right-handed objects to left-handed use, and

sometimes having to use my right hand — I think my brain gets confused by the switching.

oh, and cheque-books. I have real problems tearing the cheque out — but perhaps that's a good thing if it's stopped me writing cheques!

Has being left-handed held you back in life? Do you think you would have had a better job if you'd been right-handed?

I can't imagine a better job than this one. No, I don't think being left-handed has held me back but I do think it's a right-handed world and that we left-handers are compensating for that all the time, which perhaps isn't fair. On the other hand — no pun intended — look at your list of famous left-handers. Perhaps when people face barriers they try harder, become stronger… most of them. There do seem to be more left-handers are artists, musicians, architects, famous scientists…

So, do you think left-handers are better than right-handers?

No indeed, and any tendency in any group of people is only that — a tendency. It might be true — and I'm only suggesting this

as an example — that Welsh people generally are good singers, but I personally am tone deaf! I really believe it is up to every individual to make the most of his or her own life, whatever the talents and whatever the weaknesses.

So, you see left-handedness as a weakness?

I most definitely do not. I do however think a left-hander can feel disadvantaged. As I say, it's a right-handed world.

Does that mean you support THE AFAN TIMES campaign against prejudice towards left-handers?

I am delighted that you are challenging prejudice of whatever kind, wherever you find it. I hope you will challenge stereotypes too.

Mrs Carter, thank you so much for talking to your AFAN TIMES Reporters.

"Do you think we should put in what she said about the last article?" asked Ryan as they looked back over the interview.

"What, about how good it was?"

"No–" Ryan saw Jamie's expression and amended hastily, "that is, it was good, you know it was, and she did say, but," he hesitated, "she also said that maybe we'd got it wrong, and all those bad meanings of left were from right-handers thinking their left hand was useless and clumsy, not to do with left-handers at all."

Jamie shrugged. "Same difference. 'Gauche' still means 'left' and 'clumsy'."

"Yes but–" Ryan started then changed it to, "OK, people can think for themselves. Let's work on the new stuff." They looked again at the interview.

"Should we say, "Over and out," or something."

"That's television. This is supposed to be writing."

"But it's from talking."

"That's to give it personality, her personality." He contemplated the Head's words. "Scary woman."

"Ry, why were you surprised, really, when she started talking about all those tools?"

"Well, weren't you?"

"That's not the point. You haven't answered the question."

"I'm not stupid enough to do that, am I!"

Jamie was being hurried down the stairs and out of the house, when Ryan's mother popped out of the living room to say goodbye. Ryan clearly wanted Jamie to go but she resisted his pressure, irritated at the way he couldn't get on with his mother. What she wouldn't do for a mother as glamorous as this one, giving her total attention. She turned her most charming smile on Ryan's Mum.

"Thank you for having me, Mrs Anderson. I'm just going now."

"No problem, hon. I know Ryan's going to miss you, and you two should take some time together before we go. Why, I'll bet you even stay in touch. Night, hon."

Ryan bundled Jamie and her fading smile out of the front door, shutting it behind him so he could face her in private.

"Go? Where?" she accused him.

"America?"

"When."

"Don't know. I was going to tell you."

"Oh yeah. When? Send me a postcard?"

"I was hoping she'd change her mind."

"What about the campaign?"

"Is that all you're worried about?"

"Ryan, you're letting a draught in," called his mother.

"Bitch," Ryan muttered and, for once, Jamie was inclined to agree with him.

"Talk to you in school tomorrow," he pleaded.

Jamie shrugged. What difference would it make? Her shoulders drooped as she turned towards home. She didn't even notice the rain start.

CHAPTER 7

Jamie and Ryan had little chance to talk privately. To their amazement, the corridors swarmed with kids, especially the Year Sevens, making left-handed salutes. Ryan was in his element, turning his salute into a rhythmic step as he danced them along to class. Jamie felt like the Queen as she clapped her own shy left hand against her chest, overwhelmed at what she'd started.

There was even a good-humoured sprinkling of salutes in their own classroom. Kelly turned her back as they came in, and Jamie made a mental note that the time was coming to deal with that one. For now, she was having fun. She could almost forget that Ryan had told her he was leaving.

"I can't believe there are so many left-handers in the school," she told him.

"There aren't. This is a large enough sample to reflect the population as a whole, which means there are about 10% left-handers."

Her jaw dropped. "I won't miss you."

He grinned and for a moment the world was right again. "And more boys than girls. Which means that there's a load of deeply generous right-handers like me taking on the cause of our disadvantaged brothers and sisters."

"Glory-hunting."

"Fighting for justice."

"Using the power of the free press."

"Using your friends to get a good story."

"Telling the truth to the world."

"Your truth."

"Yours too."

"Do you always have to have the last word?"

"You just did."

"What?"

"Had the last word."

"Now you just did."

Within a week, he had gone.

"When's the next edition coming out?" some unknown kid asked Jamie, giving her the left-handed salute, which she returned automatically. It was strange the way people knew who she was. Obviously, the salute was one give-away but half the school was walking lop-sided as they swung their left arms into action; it had been Ryan who marked her out. Everyone in the school recognized Ryan; he stood out like... like Ryan. And just because she was beside him, everyone knew who she was.

"Soon," she responded listlessly. The interview with the

Head had been returned, with no changes, and was ready for press. She wandered along to see Mr Travis.

"Got this for you Sir," she held out the print-out and the USB drive. His eyebrows veed below a wrinkled forehead.

"Sorry Jamie, bad timing. Stress. Don't expect you to understand but I've been told to get a life and I'm going to be in deep deep... manure if I don't start now, and that means no school magazine for two months. I'm cutting it to one a term so you can leave it with me or bring it back next term."

Jamie folded the paper and put it back in her pocket with the USB drive.

"Jamie?" Mr Travis gave her a left-handed salute. "Well done."

She raised her left hand but it flopped back weakly. Her heart wasn't in it.

Break and lunch-times were the worst. What did you do without a friend? She tried to think back. What had she done before Ryan came? She remembered following her brother around, and spying on him round corners, giggling with some girls she had known in Juniors. It was embarrassing to think how she had behaved then. She had been so much younger.

The kids she had hung round with had changed, and she didn't have anything in common with them now. She tried having lunch in the canteen, but looking around at the groups laughing and chatting only made her feel worse. She couldn't muscle in on someone else's friend.

Kelly's loud, "Where's your boyfriend then?" as she sniggered with Donna, settled it. Jamie didn't even sit down but had took her burger outside to eat, leaning against the wall in the freezing wind.

She started going out into town at lunch-time. The school was in the town's shopping precinct, and as soon as the bell went, uniforms darkened the streets, formed queues in every fast food shop and bakery, huddled outside by the river in fine weather, and in the arcade when it was cold or wet.

Jamie often hung over the bridge, thinking. There were three trashed shopping trolleys creating eddies in the swollen river, and she could see drifts of cigarette smoke from the kids under the arches and from the council workers outside their office block. Once she saw a large black bird flying down the river, gleaming wet. One of the teachers said there was a cormorant lived on a lamp-post above the motorway, towards Briton Ferry, but she wouldn't know a cormorant if it pecked her on the nose.

She knew a cat when she saw one, though, and it made her smile to see a black-and-white cat hanging around the Post Office, miawling, while the little kids bawled at their parents for a ride on Postman Pat's van. The real-life Jess prowled the

Town Centre with the swagger of a local.

She tried going to the library where she could use the computers and work in peace, but it only left her evenings emptier. She visited her mother on the supermarket checkout, but she didn't know what to say to her and, after the first time, her mother was impatient, worried about her boss noticing the distraction.

Turfed out of Tesco, the first person she saw was the familiar figure of *The Big Issue* seller. What would her mother know about anything, she thought as she defied clear instructions about strange men and struck up a conversation. The man flinched as she reached into her pocket and dug out the coins she felt she owed him in order to talk at all. When she held out the money, he seemed to relax. As if *she* might have hurt *him*!

"How's it going?" she asked.

He gave her the magazine then rubbed his hands together in their fingerless, black, woolly gloves. "Cold. Stood here for two hours selling nothing, then three of you come along together. Worth it, see, if you just stick at it." His smile shamed her. She would have bought another *Big Issue* if she hadn't thought it might hurt his pride.

"How are *you*?" he asked.

He was the first human being to have asked her how she was, in the whole eternity of endless days since Ryan had gone. She met his eyes, brown, honest. "Awful. My best friend went to America."

He ducked his head, looked away from her. "Bad that."

So simple, the truth. If only her mother could have said, "Bad that," instead of telling her that they could email each other, that she should mix with other people, that friends came and went when you were growing up.

"Yes." She turned to go. "What's your name anyway?"

"Keith."

"I'm Jamie."

"You take care now, Jamie."

"Yeah, and you, Keith. See ya."

She went back to school, scuffing her shoes, having exhausted all possible lunch-time activities during the forever of eleven friendless schooldays, but she couldn't quite recapture her previous self-pity. Not when she knew there was a man called Keith who stood freezing on a street corner and was grateful when three people each gave him one a couple of pounds. Perhaps she would write articles for *The Big Issue*. They might be interested in the truth about left-handers, even if Mr Travis was too busy with his mid-life crisis.

It was during History that she had her idea. They were studying the evidence as to whether some tolls were a good idea and whether a bunch of Welshmen were right to dress up as women, the 'Rebeccas', and go rioting. Miss Hutchings was talking about the different evidence they had to read.

"And B is an extract from a pamphlet, a sort of newsletter that was distributed by street sellers or pamphleteers. These pamphlets were often full of criticisms of authority," Like *The Big Issue*, Jamie thought, "and published unofficially by printers who could never be caught by the newly formed police force."

The teacher was holding up a large tea-stained sheet "If it was just printed on one side of big paper like this, it would be called a broadsheet." The voice droned on in the background but it had given Jamie her idea.

When she reached home after school, which was always earlier these days, Jamie rushed upstairs. She was in luck and found it empty, so she logged on and found mail – there could only be one sender.

It couldn't be worse. Two weeks without a computer, imprisoned with an insane woman who wants me to call her 'Mom', swing on the front porch with her and bring home 'some of the guys'. The house is OK, all painted wood and creaks a lot, and there really is a front porch up some wooden steps with a kind of railing around, and this naff swinging wooden seat which my mother thinks encourages deep, meaningful, mother-son conversations. Vomit.

I was just getting used to the sweat and the bugs – more of both than you could ever imagine. I don't want to imagine what it'll be like in the summer. Cockroaches are evil. It's not so much when you see them scurrying off – they don't like light so if you shine a torch under the front porch, where there's this sort of dark hole under a platform, you see bugs everywhere – it's the sounds they make, clicking scrunching thin-hard-shell noises. Anyway, just when I'd started walking around without screaming, I had to go to school.

Mom insisted on going with me – can you imagine? So, she had the usual trouble with the car, says she's got used to a gearshift and driving on the left (and too fast – they drive more slowly here, but that's another story) and then we had to go into this huge entrance, more like the museums when I lived in London, past this bloke carrying a gun. Yes, that's what I said, there's this security guard at the school entrance wearing a gun-belt and tapping the holster as all the kids go past. Bit of a change from our lollipop-man don't you think? Same sort of personality though – growly on the surface and soft inside (apart from the gun) I just stared at that gun all the way in but the other kids didn't seem to notice at all, nor did my mother.

Then it was the usual stuff with different names, meet the Principal, do a test, join a grade, get a locker, smiley-first-day talk from teachers, serious who-the-hell-are-you stares from the bad guys. I don't want to go through all this again. Do you remember Darren? All the kids here, and all the teachers, are black, but I stick out like a sore thumb. Ironic, huh?

I'm going to send you an article about the brain and left-handedness. I'm relying on you to get my pieces published back home. I'm going to think of something that will get me back to Port Talbot as soon as I can manage. Keep me sane. Mail me something to think about.

Ryan.

Darren? Oh yes, Jamie remembered Darren. When Ryan first came to the school, some kid had overheard Ryan's mother telling the Head, "We've just moved here from London, England," and they were all tamping mad at someone thinking the Welsh were so thick they needed to be told where London was. There had been a few knives out when Ryan joined their class but the sharpest had been from Darren when the teacher announced innocently, "This is Ryan from London."

"Is that London, England, or London, Africa?"

"What do you mean?" The teacher had known enough not to play but not enough to understand the game.

Others had carefully rescued Darren. "You know, like there's a Bethlehem in Wales and a Bethlehem... somewhere else." Their Geography was not as clever as their intentions but served its purpose.

Darren clung to the 'London, England' for months, long after Ryan became himself to the other kids, and her best friend to Jamie. However much Ryan was pestered, the way he just showed interest in humans as a species was just too much, even for Darren, in the end. Jamie could imagine Ryan turning that same scientific interest on the bugs.

Fired up again for her campaign, Jamie went back to her own room to dig out the interview with the Head and her research notes. A movement outside the window caught her eye. Kelly, sneaking into the yard! She had a score to settle there, and once she finished mailing Ryan, with all her new article attached, she would go down to the coal shed and sort that Kelly out.

CHAPTER 8

The television was blaring in the living room, with both her parents splayed in front of it, recovering from one day's work before facing the next. Jamie went past unnoticed and out the back door. She steeled herself for the blast of sentimental lyrics but all was surprisingly quiet in the coal shed. Too quiet.

Prepared to find no one there, Jamie pushed open the door. Gareth was humming softly to himself, trying to manage a pencil, a piece of paper and a can on the chair between his thighs. As Jamie watched, he lost the battle to keep them all on the chair, and it was the can which toppled, spilling beer down his trousers and onto the floor. Gareth hardly noticed.

"Jamie," he slurred, "Wanna beer?" He picked up the can from the floor and passed it to her.

"If you can spare it." She looked at the empty can but her sarcasm was wasted on her sozzled brother.

"S'all right," he told her generously, "I can get another one," and, true to his words, he staggered to a corner, lifted a scruffy bomber jacket and pulled out another can from the pile stashed underneath. He made it safely back to his chair, where he conducted his renewed humming by waving alternately his pencil and his can. There was a small pile of ring-pulls below his chair.

"You're pissed." Jamie informed him, and was rewarded with an idiotic smile.

"Jus' happy."

The empties were stacked as a small tower, and two of the band were bowling another crumpled empty at the pile, to see how many they could knock down in one go, then repeating the whole process, which they seemed to find very entertaining. As the cans were dented by the game, as more were added, and as the boys' alcohol content grew, they found it increasingly difficult to stack the pile. This apparently made the game even more entertaining, rather than less. As if, Jamie thought, this lot needed any chemical help to turn their brains to jelly.

Another pile of coats on the floor had been wriggling and squealing while Jamie observed the general scene. Two heads emerged, and Jamie identified the red, flustered face of Kelly, being smothered in sticky kisses by an equally red-faced Chris, who was muttering the time-honoured Port Talbot endearment, "Come y'ere, you."

Kelly vanished again beneath the coat, like someone drowning. Some sixth sense prevented Jamie from politely looking the other way, just leaving, and taking up her quarrel with Kelly at a more convenient time. She couldn't have said what it was, but there was something wrong with the way the coats wriggled, not just like someone drowning, but like kittens struggling to survive when someone was drowning them. That did it. If she was mistaken, she'd look a fool, but if she wasn't…

Jamie kicked the struggling coats. "Oy, Kelly, you all right?"

Two faces surfaced for air, speaking at the same time.

"Leave us alone. Want a bit of privacy." But it wasn't Chris that Jamie heard, it was Kelly's choked, "No, get me out… help me."

Chris was beyond subtlety so Jamie aimed a couple more kicks at the coats earning groans from both the inmates as she found soft targets.

"Sorry," she said, and kicked them again, as she pulled the coats off to reveal two tangled humans. An electric lightbulb has a curiously calming effect on romance, and it became easy enough to pull Kelly away from the somewhat dazed band member. Jamie recognised the bomber jacket covering the beers as belonging to Kelly and draped it round her classmate, who was huddled on the floor with her head on her knees, and her arms round them.

Chris staggered over to stand within inches of the two of them, towering over them both, glaring, balling his hands into fists and smacking one hand into the other. Kelly didn't even look up, and Jamie said not a word, which was probably what saved the situation.

"Just so you know, right?" Chris stated and it seemed enough for him to feel he had salvaged his pride. He lumbered away from them to the beer corner, opened a can and poured the whole contents over his head.

"Cool!" observed one of the bowling boys, grabbing a can and following suit.

Jamie addressed her grinning brother. "Gareth! There's going to be hell to pay if Mum and Dad catch you. I'm walking Kelly home. Get this load of idiots out of here and I'll help you clear up when I come back."

"Mum an' Dad," Gareth repeated, the dawning of some forgotten danger in his eyes, "Mum an' Dad…"

Jamie shrugged. If he was past it, there was nothing she could do. First, she was going to see Kelly got home safely.

What was she doing walking the yellow-lit streets arm-in-arm with her worst enemy? For once it was clear and dry but, if there were stars above, they couldn't pierce the town's personal cloud cover. Kelly unhooked her arm.

"I'm OK. I only had a can or two – not like them – I was just joining in."

"I didn't know you were going out with Chris."

"I'm not."

"So?"

"I can sing." It was the simplest, most revealing statement Jamie had ever heard. "I'd do anything to get into a band."

Jamie pictured the wrestling coats.

"No, not 'anything'," Kelly admitted ruefully. "I knew he fancied me, see, and I thought if I let him think I fancied him back, then maybe he'd ask Gareth if I could sing a bit for them, but he'd drunk a bit..."

"Why didn't you just ask Gareth?"

"Don't be dull, girl, Gareth's too much above me, like. I mean he writes the songs... and that voice on him... he'd never look at someone like me."

Jamie struggled to come to terms with this view of her brother. "He's just ordinary, you know. Bit of a pain mostly."

"Him, ordinary? I'd sit in that shed for hours, just to hear him."

Oh, no. For hou-urs, waiting for flow-ers no doubt. It wasn't only alcohol that did kids' brains in. They walked on a bit without speaking.

Then Kelly said quietly, "I was so scared. I couldn't have stopped him. That's not what I want."

"I know. It's just drink, makes them stupid. Make you stupid too, if you did join in," she couldn't resist adding.

"I'm not that stupid. Tried it once, puked all next day, and what a headache. Don't like the way other people are one up on you when you've drunk too much. You can't trust anyone," she said bitterly.

"You should have remembered that tonight," Jamie

needled, hating herself and sounding like her mother. "It's not just whether *you* drink too much – it's what *they* do."

"Oh, like you're always such a saint!"

"No, just some of us don't have to do something to find out it's stupid. It's called thinking."

"Well, thanks for the lesson!" They were silent again.

"You don't like me, do you."

"Why should I?"

"So why did you help me?"

"That's different. Not liking is personal. *That* was disgusting!"

In a very small voice, Kelly said, "I'm trying to say thank you. You always make it so hard, don't you. It was the same when I tried to say sorry for dropping you in it with Davies. But no, you come out smelling of roses and lovey-dovey with the Head. I don't know how you do it. You walk round school as if you and that Ryan own the universe and you make the rest of us feel thick."

"Forget it." Jamie had been given too much to think about for one night.

Kelly gathered up her hurt pride. "I'll be fine from here. That's my house by there." She hesitated. "You won't say in school, will you?"

"What do you think I am?"

Kelly opened her mouth to speak and Jamie jumped in

quickly. "No, don't answer that. Well, you're wrong. Perhaps we're both wrong." A thought struck her. "No-one's above you."

"Didn't feel like that earlier this evening."

"You know what I mean. It's a bad way of thinking."

"Yes. Thank you."

They parted awkwardly, unable to say the cheerful 'Seeya' of friendship but brought close enough to feel the need. Jamie turned and plodded a silent way home, nearly reaching it safely.

"Oh no," she groaned as a lanky figure stumbled towards her along the otherwise empty street.

Ryan had just arrived home from school and ran to the friendship of his computer. He typed,

```
Toilets were bad in Afan, but I aint seen
nothing like this. There's wacky-baccy smelly
smoke hanging over cubicles with a minimum of
five legs in each one (Don't ask - I haven't
figured it out yet but I'm sure it's biolog-
ical in some way I don't want to know). Some
seriously hard dudes keep watch and I have
the feeling it's not a place to be caught
with your pants down, which makes the busi-
ness in hand kind of difficult if you know what
```

I mean. And no way am I revealing any of my bits out in the open, so the only thing for it is to go all day without going all day. I'm training now.

Not wearing uniform is such a good idea, and there's none of that fuss about boys' hair being too long, too short, too hairy... Some of the girls — and some of the boys for that matter — have great crinkly hairdos with beads and wrappers but I can't give you the technical low-down. No-one seems to worry what colour hair is either — there's blonde streaks and the usual changers like at home who are purple one day, red the next.

Here, no one wastes time arguing about how you look, which is great. The downside is that you can tell straight off who the gangs are — and there's a lot of pressure on what you wear to show who you're with. So far, I've kept up with the "Me new boy, no dress sense" but I'm getting a lot of advice on how to wise up, what music T-shirts to wear or whatever, a lot of pressure. The shape of my trousers — sorry, 'pants' — seems to insult a lot of kids.

I've made some sort-of friends, and I don't know what to do about them. They found out that I know about computers so they hang round me to see if I'll find out some stuff for them. As these are some of the heavies who keep watch round the toilets, you can imagine

the sort of stuff they want me to find out –
how to make a bomb, gun specs and so on.

They are real posers, even wear gangster
coats and dark glasses. I'm sending you an
article for the campaign and then I'm going
to surf some terrorist sites for my new
'friends'. I'm starting to get an idea on
how I can back to Port Talbot sooner rather
than later.

Forgot to tell you, I've been told to use American spellings so I'm learning the language!
I was OK with words like program, color and
meter but I cannot believe 'ax' or 'check'
instead of 'cheque', or 'sulfur'! Seriously!
If you were here, I'd sure nuff whoop your
sorry bad-ass.

Also, almost – but not quite – as bad as the
toilets, is what they call 'sport'. Please!
They call it 'football' – some excuse for the
class morons to charge at me wearing full
armour plating and helmets. Basketball is not
so bad – they tell me I have bounce. Did you
ever notice that? If I stay here much longer
my mother will be lining up cheerleaders for
me to choose from – you can see your face
in their teeth and they're a bit short in
the brains department. Speaking of which...
enjoy the virtual brain surgery (magazine
article attached).

Ryan.

IF YOU'RE IN YOUR RIGHT MIND, YOU'RE PROBABLY LEFT-HANDED

Everyone has a brain divided into two halves.

Each half has different talents.

The two halves usually work together in any activity but one can dominate.

BRAINS AND BODIES ARE CROSS-WIRED
so that ...

* the left side of your brain is in charge of the right side of your body,

* and the right side of your brain is in charge of the left side of your body.

This means that the right brain is usually in charge of left-handers

QUIZ

WHICH DO YOU REMEMBER BETTER
a) people's names? OR
b) people's faces?

DO YOU FIND IT EASIER TO
a) sing a song along to the music? OR
b) give instructions to someone?

WHEN YOU HAVE A PUZZLE TO SOLVE, DO YOU PREFER TO
a) have something you can see and move about to try answers? OR
b) talk your way to an answer (to yourself or with someone else)?

ARE YOU MORE LIKELY TO
a) get lost? OR
b) lose track of time?

WOULD YOU RATHER EXPLAIN SOMETHING WITH
a) objects, pictures, a visual display, something to show? OR
b) with words?

Every a) answer is using the right side of your brain;

every b) answer is using the left side of your brain.

If we could always use whichever side of our brain is best for the task in hand, we would be brilliant, but one side tends to dominate and can spoil what we're trying to do.

If you're trying to learn a song, the right side of the brain will do it so much better if the left side is not talking to itself saying, "The first word is I, the next word is am, then so, oh yes, so that's 'I am so in love with you."

The right side of the brain doesn't know how it learns, it just does;

it gets you to school because you recognise the way, without having to say "I turn left at my gate, then I have to turn left again..."

However, the left side of the brain helps you learn the vocabulary and grammar of a new language, while the right side just hears and copies it as a different sort of music.

The left side also tells you when it's time to take a break, whereas your right side leaves you in that daydream where you say, "Is that the time — I'm starving!"

IS IT DIFFERENT FOR GIRLS?

Tests have shown that when they solve problems, women often use both halves of their brain whereas men generally only use one half.

This supports the theory that women tend to be better at multi-tasking.

It could also explain why men tend to be better at solving problems where they can see or move objects (right brain) because they don't let the left brain interfere.

One experiment showed that, in Maths tests, left-handed males generally performed best.

If you're using both halves of your brain, then words and language (left brain) always play a part in solving problems. Sometimes this is helpful; sometimes we need to tell the left brain to SHUT UP!

CHAPTER 9

It was inevitable that Chris would lurch towards Jamie, looming and threatening in the empty street. In the pale glow of the street lights, his face looked even paler, but his eyes were more inhabited than earlier in the evening, when Jamie could see no one at home – certainly no one she could talk to. His voice also sounded steadier. He stank of stale beer, and his hair was spiking in sticky clumps where he'd poured the can contents over his head. Jamie didn't like to contemplate what the flecks on his face might be.

"You." He jabbed her ribs, blocking her escape route, "shouldn't have interfered."

"You," she toughed it out, echoing his tone and staring up at him, "were too drunk to know what you were doing. You seem a bit better now."

"Puked my guts up," he acknowledged.

Jamie grimaced. "Hope it wasn't in our yard."

"Round the corner," he grinned, and the pointing finger dropped to his side. "Was the little tart a friend of yours or what?"

"Seems to me you're the little tart," Jamie fired back, "You're the one who doesn't care who you're with, once you've had a bit. Don't you even know her name?" Had she gone too far?

The drink hadn't worn off enough for Chris to find thinking easy but at least that was what he was trying to do. This wasn't the animal of earlier on, this was a mate of her brother's, a bit the worse for too much to drink. How could he have behaved like that?

"No," he said finally. "What's her name?"

"Kelly," Jamie said, "and I bet she'll remember your name all right. You're lucky if she doesn't go to the police, the way you behaved. It's sexual assault, that's what it is. For your information, she's in my class at school."

If Chris could have looked greener, he would have.

"Your class," he repeated.

"Yes, so that's how I know her."

"Your class."

"I said so, didn't I."

"But you're just a kid, Gareth's kid sister."

"Thank you so much!"

"But she looks... up for it. The skirt... And you're saying this...oh shit... this Kelly... is the same age as you?"

"Quick tonight, aren't you! Kelly's been coming along to hear the band for weeks now, and you don't know the first thing about her except she's not strong enough to fight you off when you fancy a grope. You're disgusting!"

"I didn't know."

"Well you know now." Jamie tried to stay outraged but she

could see in his eyes that he was more disgusted with himself than she could ever make him. "I'm off," she shrugged and walked past him without any attempt to stop her on his part.

Next door's big ginger tom was wailing on the wall, serenading an imaginary moon, and Jamie stopped to clear her head. The cat had other things on his mind but he bowed his head for her to rub behind his ears before she unlatched the gate to the back yard, just as her father appeared at the back door to shout at the tom. It was one of those nights.

"Jamie? What the hell you doing out so late?"

"Went to a friend's." *Keep your head down and say as little as possible.* There wasn't any sign of light or sound in the coal shed, and Jamie tried the door surreptitiously as she passed – it was locked.

"I don't know what's got into you, my girl, you know you're not allowed out this late, and on a school night. You can forget going anywhere the next two weeks – you're grounded. You should be more like your brother. He's been in his bed over an hour. Get to your room, you."

"Yes, Dad. Sorry, Dad." She hadn't wanted to go anywhere anyway.

She knocked quietly on Gareth's bedroom door but there was no response, which was hardly surprising, given the state he'd been in when she'd last seen him. She'd play sick in the morning, and the two of them would clear up when Mum and Dad were at work. Her brother owed her, big-time, and she had the germ of an idea for how he could pay her back.

When they had finished swilling out the floor in the coal shed the next morning, and dumped all the empty beer cans in the wheelie bin at the end of the street (Gareth's job so no nosy neighbour would snitch on Jamie for not being as ill as she'd made out), Jamie told her brother she was going to use the computer. She took his groan as assent and grinned.

It had not been difficult to convince her mother that they both had some stomach bug, not with Gareth in residence in the bathroom, and looking deathly when he emerged. A few weak little words from Jamie had given them both the day at home with their mother's blessing. Gareth had known better than to cry off the cleaning up, but it had certainly not helped the delicate state of his head and stomach, and he made frequent disappearances throughout the morning, much to Jamie's malicious delight.

The mail from Ryan gave her pause, and then she started her reply.

Don't think you're impressing me, good boy. We got school toilets and drugs here you know, it's just we don't do the latter in the former. As you very well know, there's no need for those kids stupid enough to do drugs to do them in school; everyone knows where to hang out round town if that's what they want. And when we get a new boy here, we do welcome him proper, see, so he do talk tidy, so don't you give me none of your bad-ass talk. Guns is different. You want to keep well clear of those new 'friends' of yours. Too trusting, you are.

I don't know how to ask this without sounding bad but you know when you were here, didn't you sometimes feel odd being the only black kid in school? I mean, you say you feel more out of place now but you had to put up with some stupid things in school, didn't you?

Like that teacher who kept mentioning how great Martin Luther King was, every time she saw you. As if that's the only famous black guy she's ever heard of. Come to think of it, were there any other famous black guys? (Just joking)

And all the snide little remarks, like Mrs Davies' "I'd have thought you'd know about important prejudice." It must feel good to be out of all that.

I'll be honest, I'd be scared if I was in the school you're in now, the only white kid, but when you were the only black kid, you were just... you. How come we never talked about this when you were here? How come we talked about me being left-handed?

Anyway, I've had the most amazing nearly-awful night - you wouldn't believe the mess Kelly got herself into - and I've got some plans for the campaign so keep sending me more stuff.

There was something calming about writing to Ryan, not as good as seeing him but it helped her think and put her in the mood for campaign work. His piece about the brain would please the Head and go well with the interview, and, when she'd finished her own articles, the broadsheet was ready to run.

FORGET THE ROMANS ...

NEANDERTHALS (STONE AGE) made both left-handed and right-handed tools in apparently equal numbers.

THE ANCIENT GREEKS wrote alternately left to right and right to left like ploughing a field, they called it 'boustrophedon'.

you could read it this way
yaw siht ti daer dluoc uoy dna

They thought that people should try to be AMBIDEXTROUS.

THE ANCIENT EGYPTIANS wrote every which way, left, right, top, bottom. They also believed that the 'vena amoris' (vein of love) ran from the heart to the 3rd finger of the left hand, which is probably why many cultures still use that finger for a wedding ring. Just as well modern surgeons don't use other beliefs from ancient Egypt.

CHINESE SCRIPT goes from top to bottom and right to left.

THE INCAS thought it was lucky to be left-handed and one of their great chiefs was called Lloque Yupanqui(it means 'the left-handed').

HINDUS circle something 3 times from left to right to purify it.

ARABIC writing goes from right to left and traditionally, Arabs tend to write with their left hands. The bad news is that they are also supposed to use their left hands for cleaning unmentionable parts of the body (They are supposed to eat with their right hands).

According to THE BOOK OF JUDGES IN THE BIBLE (generally a very depressing book for left-handers), the Israelites were defeated by an elite army chosen from thousands of 'the children of Benjamin', consisting of '700 chosen men who were left-handed; every one could sling stones at a hair's breadth, and not miss'.

A SCOTTISH CLAN, THE KERRS, contained so many left-handers that they built their castle stairways to spiral up anticlockwise, giving left-handers at the top of the stairs the advantage.

According to some evidence, at the time the USA was colonised, 1 in 3 native Americans was left-handed.

CELEBRATE TUESDAYS!

Tuesday is named after the left-handed Scandinavian god, Tiw.

The next day, when she returned to school, Jamie responded with a vague smile to Kelly's pleading glance. She had almost forgotten about Kelly, in her plans for advancing the cause of left-handers. At lunch-time, she rushed along to the computer room, caught the IT teacher before he locked up and explained that Mr Travis had said she could save him the work and print out the next copy of the school magazine herself. She waved her USB drive at him, and, although he took a lot of convincing that her drive didn't carry every virus in the known universe, she put on her most honest expression until he gave in.

It was easy to look honest because although it wasn't exactly what Mr Travis had said, it was what he had implied he wanted. He'd said he was overworked, he'd said he liked what she and Ryan had written, so it was logical to think he'd be pleased if she got on with it herself, printing a good old-fashioned anti-authority broadsheet. As an English teacher, he'd always gone on about them reading between the lines, reading the subtext and using inference, so she had inferred what he really wanted.

Half an hour and 1000 sheets of A3 paper later, there was a special broadsheet edition of *The Afan Times* (printed small in one corner), under the new banner:

ON THE OTHER HAND

Red-faced but satisfied, Jamie called into a Year 7 classroom as soon as the bell went for afternoon registration; you could rely on the littluns to do jobs – they were still keen. She gave the salute and chose the ten keenest in responding to distribute her newspaper 'from Mr Travis.' She had something special planned for the 300 copies she had kept in her bag.

SO HOW DO YOU KNOW IF YOU'RE LEFT-HANDED?

Most people use both hands to some extent and it's not as simple as saying that you're left-handed only if you write with your left hand.

TAKE THE TORQUE TEST

Draw lots of Xs on a page, then draw a circle round each one swapping back and fore between your left hand and your right hand for each circle. Which way round did you draw the circles, clockwise (the way the clock goes round, right to left)?

or anticlockwise

(the opposite way, left to right)?

WHICH HAND?

The hand you use to do these *tasks* is likely to be *your dominant hand*:

comb hair, deal cards, strike a match, pet the dog, open a door, brush teeth, pour water from a jug, catch a ball, thread a needle, hammer a nail, use a mouse

IF YOU DO ALL THIS WITH YOUR LEFT HAND BUT WRITE WITH YOUR RIGHT, you were probably forced to write right-handed but you are a natural left-hander

RESULTS OF THE TORQUE TEST

clockwise is natural to a right-hander

anticlockwise is natural to a left-hander —

left-handers sometimes read a clock the 'opposite' way round so that 1.20 is seen as 10.40. You can buy left-handed clocks which are read anticlockwise

CLOCKWISE

ANTICLOCKWISE

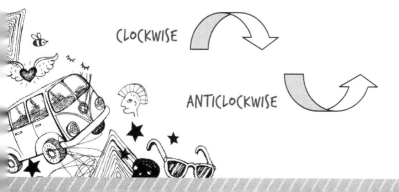

CHAPTER 10

Great stuff, Jamie. I loved *On the Other Hand*. What's with all the hard questions you're asking me though – you keep your reporter's habits away from me! As soon as you start asking how it feels to be black, I worry about you. You're worse than Mom wanting me to get in touch with my 'roots'. I have no idea how it feels to be black. I've always been black. I don't wake up each morning thinking 'Hey I'm black' any more than it's a surprise to you to be a girl – it's normal. Anyway there's too much to tell you to think about that any more.

The men in black have given me toilet privileges for the class computer work I've done for them. This means that my mean-dude friends insist on me being first in a cubicle and they hover in a visually threatening way, muttering, "Don't mess with him, man" or "he's with us" as soon as anyone looks at me. This cuts me off from anyone I might be able to have a reasonable conversation with, but it'll be worth it when I let Mom see my new friends.

I'm ready for the next part of my plan –

before I go crazy hanging out with these creeps. I thought of leaving the print-outs lying round so she could find the ingredients and instructions for making a bomb, specs for various guns, pictures of bullet wounds relating impact pattern to weapon used, and a few other of their fantasy research proj-ects. I don't think that would do it though. Mum would probably just shout at me and throw them away.

But if I can get the men in black to call round to collect their print-outs and I can let a few select picture pages (with some gory colour bits on them) drop so that some get found later... I reckon I'll be back in Port Talbot before you can say, Myrddyn.

Which reminds me, I've told the men in black that I was in a hell's angel chapter in the UK (sorry – if I say Wales – they say "Where?", I explain, they say "Oh, Wales, England, why didn't you say..." and it's all too tedious so I just say UK or England – I know I'll pay for that when I come back to Wales but that's just how it is. You can't fight all the people all the time.)

Anyway, I told them I was in this hell's angel chapter (and they believed me – told you IQ was an issue!) and as they were my brothers I'd tell them my initiated name. You'd have died laughing — they were so impressed — and I bet you can guess my secret name, can't you.

You're right — the men in black think Myrddin is a rock-hard biker name! One-nil to Wales! I hope that makes up for giving in over saying UK. I've been wondering about showing them the rituals of the inner circle (Eisteddfod ceremonies would do nicely) but it's a bit dodgy round here to suggest dressing up in robes (even you must have heard of the Klu Klux Klan, and its not a joke in people's memories here) and I just can't see the guys doing the flower dance or competing for the bardic crown.

Funny how people are sensitive about different things in different places; if I say 'boy' like we would in a friendly way back home, someone's fit to kill me, and I finally worked out that it's a black thing — in slave and ex-slave times, all black men were called 'Boy' by whites, so it's an insult here, like saying you think you're superior. I've heard your Dad saying, "He's a boy," about one of his mates, or that he was going out with the boys — that would not go down well here.

I told you I've got bounce, well, Mom and some journalist friend took me to see the

Hawks play basketball. I tell you, there was a pass and a slam-dunk in the last three seconds of the first half and the way this guy moved down the court – poetry! I think I'm finally hooked.

Bring Kelly out here with you and the two of you can be cheerleaders for me while I play. Let me hear you... "Give us an R – R! Give us a Y – Y!" You get the idea – a bit of practice and you could manage four letters while Kelly shakes her booty.

I'm being threatened with a baseball match some time. A whole day watching men play rounders – sounds really exciting. The only interesting thing about the game is to do with left-handers – see new article attached.

LEFT-HANDER?

In the United States, you'd be called a Southpaw

Baseball is *THE* national game in the States.

In baseball, it's a real advantage to be left-handed. When you're pitching, you can surprise the hitter and keep an eye on first base at the same time; when you're hitting, you have the advantage against a right-handed pitcher.

LEFT-HANDED BASEBALL PLAYERS ARE CALLED 'SOUTHPAWS' because in 1890 in the baseball diamond in Chicago pitchers faced west so the hitters didn't have to face afternoon sunshine. This meant that a pitcher's left-hand was to the south, hence a left-hander was called a 'Southpaw'.

The term is used widely in the States to describe a left-hander.

The BASEBALL HALL OF FAME includes Super-Southpaw Babe Ruth.

20% of pitchers in the Hall of Fame are Southpaws.

1 in 3 US Presidents is a Southpaw, including

JAMES GARFIELD, whose party trick was to write in Greek with his left hand at the same time as writing in Latin with his right — beat that!

GERALD FORD, who is only left-handed when he sits down. When he stands up he throws a ball, writes and plays golf right-handed!

Atlanta sure has some grand buildings – in fact, grand everything – shopping, leisure, food – but I wish they didn't package everything, just let me think for myself. I do like the way American cities are so organised – streets numbered on a grid system so you can always find your way round. My mother, with and without this friend of hers, is dragging me to places "I'll just love" and I don't.

The latest was this theme park, 'Six Flags Over Georgia', where I suffered Batman the Ride in the company of my screaming mother and a load of screaming kids. I do not understand the attraction of wandering through a plastic 'Gotham City' admiring Batman's crime-fighting devices, then imposing unnecessary and unpleasant g-force (allegedly 4Gs and speeds of up to 50mph) on your churning stomach, confirming the effects of blood rushing dangerously to the brain, and then choosing how to answer your mother's "What did you think?"

Thinking has nothing to do with it, which is what I told her. She didn't speak to me till I'd eaten two hotdogs and said it was a great day out. I guess I'm just too old for this stuff. It could be worse. She could have taken me to Bugs Bunny World.

The teachers have started on me about being a good American; apart from the business of saluting the flag each morning, I've been given a book of facts for 'the new American'. They sure take this stuff seriously and they're really geared up for us immigrants (You ask me about feeling at home here and I'm told I'm an immigrant? I don't care how much they say America welcomes immigrants I don't want to be an immigrant at all, I want to be home).

I'm supposed to learn how many states, the names of the Presidents, names of Generals – it's a whole different general knowledge – and they have no idea about kings and queens of England, never mind things like in Wales, England there are two official languages. On the plus side, part of becoming a good American citizen was a homework 'paper' (meaning essay) on Benjamin Franklin – two birds with one stone! I have a great article for you on one of the all-time superhero left-handers. What couldn't he do?!

If you would not be forgotten
as soon as you are dead and rotten
either write things worth reading
or do things worth the writing
— Benjamin Franklin

Now I'm becoming a good American citizen, I'm having to drink less coffee. I can't figure the American attitude to coffee; there are coffee-houses on every street, selling forty different kinds of coffee in three sizes of plastic cup, and my mother gets bottomless coffee (endless free re-fills) when we eat out, but if I ask for coffee they look at me like I'm an abused child – and they look at my mother like she's the abuser.

One waitress even told me, "You're awful young to drink coffee!" Really! They're very strange about alcohol as well. You aren't an adult here till you're 21 and they're real strict about not serving alcohol to under 21s, and they insist on you showing ID so unless you've got older friends, alcohol's off-limits.

Doesn't bother me but it seems odd that you can get drugs and guns more easily than a beer. Very different from home where you have to try hard not to have alcohol poured down your throat! Liked your description of your brother's band being tanked up – glad I didn't have to clean up with you!

Shooters – it's all the men in black talk about. Their idea of a hobby is shooting something small; their idea of work would be shooting something big. Mum was advised by her colleagues on what sort of gun she should keep by her bedside 'to protect herself' and she was so shocked I thought it might be enough to get us home but no. However, it did show that she's not so keen on returning to her own roots as she thought she was. Definitely time to act on the plan. Wish me luck and hope to see you soon.

Ryan.

BENJAMIN FRANKLIN – SUPER SOUTHPAW ACHIEVEMENTS:

printer-owner of the Pennsylvania Gazette, and journalist, writing under a variety of names from the age of 15 on

joint owner with his wife of general store and book store

SCIENTIST AND INVENTOR OF:
a heat-efficient stove (the Franklin stove)
swim fins
bifocal spectacles
a glass harmonica
the lightning rod

top politician, working in England and in France.

Disenchanted with being governed by Britain, he became a father of American independence, one of those to draft and sign:

The Declaration of Independence & The Treaty of Paris

public campaigner for the abolition of slavery, for women's rights

creator of the first public library and the University of Pennsylvania

vegetarian (before the idea had been invented in the US or Europe)

a Southpaw who wrote about the importance of treating left-handers fairly

But he was definitely human.

WHAT BENJAMIN FRANKLIN MIGHT PREFER YOU DIDN'T KNOW ABOUT HIM:

HE WAS A CRIMINAL: At 17, he ran away from the beatings of his elder brother who was also his boss. Benjamin worked as an apprentice at his brother's newspaper and, despite — or perhaps because of — getting articles published under an alias, and running the paper when his brother was in prison, Benjamin was treated badly by his brother James. Running away was illegal then in America.

HE WAS A BIT OF A LAD: He met his future wife, Deborah Read, when he was 17 but, although they became sweethearts, he ran away from Deborah's hopes of marriage and she married someone else. When he was 22, he fathered a son, William, and we don't know who the mother was. Two years later, Deborah's husband had run off and Benjamin married her. Following a long marriage and Deborah's death, Benjamin became well-known in France for his enjoyment of pretty Parisiennes.

HE WAS A BIT OF A 007: From an English point of view,

Franklin was a double agent who spied on and betrayed his country (England). His son William, who was Royal Governor of New Jersey and loyal to the throne, never forgave him for this.

A Petition of the Left Hand

To Those Who Have the Superintendency of Education

There are twin sisters of us; and the two eyes of man do not more resemble, nor are capable of being upon better terms with each other, than my sister and myself, were it not for the partiality of our parents, who make the most injurious distinctions between us. From my infancy I have been led to consider my sister as being of a most elevated rank. I was suffered to grow up without the least instruction while nothing was spared in her education. She had masters to teach her writing, drawing, music and other accomplishments; but if by chance I touched a pencil, a pen, or a needle, I was bitterly rebuked; and more than once have I been beaten for being awkward and wanting a graceful manner. It is true, my sister associated me with her upon some occasions; but she always made a point of taking the lead, calling upon me only from necessity or to figure by her side...

...Condescend, sirs, to make my parents sensible of the injustice of an exclusive tenderness, and of the necessity of distributing their care and affection among their children equally. I am, with a profound respect, sirs, your obedient servant,

the Left Hand

Even though Jamie laughed at some parts, she felt uneasy as she read Ryan's account of life in Atlanta, and she couldn't explain why. It was the same nagging feeling which had made her check whether Kelly was all right under that pile of coats – a right-brain feeling with no words for it. She clicked on *Reply*, wrote,

`You take care. You're in bad company. You're too trusting and you don't know what people can be like.`

She looked at it. What a stupid thing to say – she sounded like her mother again. She deleted it, logged off and took the print-outs of Ryan's emails back to her room. If she cut out the personal bits, they would be great copy for the next broadsheet. People would be interested in what life was like in the USA. She could put in a column from *Our Correspondent in America*.

She took a highlighter out of her pencil case and used it to colour the bits she wanted to keep, adding some linking words to keep the sense. She was starting to feel the draught and, as she went to close the window, she noticed a girlish figure arrive in the yard. She hauled the window up again, smiling to herself.

"Hey, Kelly."

"Jamie." Kelly looked up sheepishly.

"What you doing here, girl? Haven't you had enough of that lot?" Jamie's tone took away the sting of the words.

"Got to keep trying. Don't worry – I won't be doing *that* again."

"If he starts anything, lamp him one."

"Sounds good to me."

Kelly gave a little wave and vanished into the coal shed. Jamie shut the window again, hoping that her no-good brother would keep his promise.

Malcolm Travis walked back to his car from the supermarket, before going home at the end of the school day. He was talking to himself, as he went through his shopping list. "Potatoes, tick, apples, tick, toilet rolls, tick, milk, tick, bread, tick," His wife would kill him if he forgot something, and he knew if he didn't double-check there would be something that appeared, as if in visible ink, to taunt him when he arrived home.

There it was – 'chicken pieces'! He could have sworn that had magically appeared on the list, in his wife's neat handwriting, after he had left the supermarket. Perhaps it was a plot to drive him insane so she would be rich, free and single. He sighed, thinking it unlikely, and he turned to go back to the supermarket to buy chicken pieces.

The man selling *The Big Issue* caught his eye – it was always reassuring to see someone worse off than you were. Although, he considered gloomily, if he offered *The Big Issue* seller a life swap, there was no guarantee the man would be delighted at facing thirty different sullen adolescents every hour, whereas a little stress-free spell selling *The Big Issue* had its attractions. As he took the magazine, a sheet fell out and he tried to hand it back.

"S'all right, boy," the man told him, "'s from the school, like, and it's free."

Mr Travis looked down at a copy of *On the Other Hand*, published – according to the information in one corner – as part of *The Afan Times*.

CHAPTER 11

"Hey Jamie, come here," a boy with short brown hair called across the canteen, so Jamie took her tray over to his table. "Gav here can't decide if he's left-handed or not." They consulted a copy of *On the Other Hand* lying on the table. "He uses his right hand for dealing cards, striking matches…"

"He gets through a few of those," someone commented.

The boy, Justin, continued his catalogue, "Petting the dog, opening the door, catching a ball, using a mouse, but he uses his left hand to comb his hair and he doesn't do any of the other things."

"Don't drink water or brush teeth," Gavin confirmed. Jamie believed him.

"We think he's been switched," Justin declared, proudly using a new term, "you know – forced right-handed."

"Well, it's possible," Jamie was cautious. "What do you think?"

"No-one's done nothing to me." Gavin didn't seem at all happy with the idea that he might turn out to be a left-hander masquerading as a right-hander.

"Show me what you do when you comb your hair," Jamie suggested. With some encouragement from his mates, Gavin took his comb out of his right trouser pocket, transferred it to his left hand, used the comb as alleged, with his left hand, while his right hand held his hair in its chosen style.

A passing teacher expressed disgust, "Not when you're eating, Gavin, for goodness' sake," and was cheerfully ignored as six pairs of eyes focused intently on Justin's behaviour. "Mr Travis was looking for you, Jamie," he added, and continued on his way to some quieter place, where teachers could lunch in peace.

"Got it!" Jamie was triumphant. "You use gel in the morning, don't you."

"What's it to you?"

"You use your dominant hand to spread the gel and hold the style."

They all nodded sagely and there was a unanimous verdict of, "Right-handed."

"Classic," declared Justin, shaking his head.

"Don't worry, Gav, you could be left-eyed or left-footed – check out the next edition." She informed them, "You've got a dominant eye and foot, not just hand."

"Bet Gavin's left-footed!" Justin stared earnestly at Gavin once more. "Thanks, Jamie."

She shrugged modestly, looked round and, aware of welcoming smiles at several tables, chose somewhere to sit and share her expertise.

SO, YOU KNOW
WHETHER YOU'RE
LEFT-HANDED WHICH PROBABLY
MEANS YOU KNOW IF YOU'RE LEFT-FOOTED?
LEFT-EYED?

Check it out...

YOU ARE LEFT-FOOTED IF YOU prefer to kick a ball, take off for a jump or hop on your left foot

TEST FOR DOMINANT EYE:

Hold your arms out and make a triangle with the index fingers and thumbs of both hands. Now frame a distant object so it is inside that triangle. Close your right eye. If the object stays in the same place, then it is our left eye which is dominant. If the object seems to move position, then it is your right eye which is dominant.

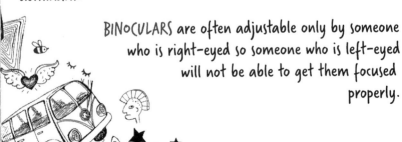

BINOCULARS are often adjustable only by someone who is right-eyed so someone who is left-eyed will not be able to get them focused properly.

Jamie tried to find Mr Travis but was told he was out of school for the afternoon. What did he want anyway? She had too much to do to wonder for long. She'd been thinking about the weird pictures in the Head's Office, and she wanted some information about Escher so she hung back after Art to talk to Mr Denning.

"Escher? Some clever tricks but merely a graphic designer," was his dampening response, so Jamie figured she'd ask their Graphic Design teacher.

At first, she'd thought he hadn't heard her, as the teacher pottered off, without a word, to the back of the room, but then he returned with paper and pencils. Definitely a right-hand brain, non-verbal type teacher, she thought, wondering what she was in for.

Mr Stevens contemplated the blank sheet of paper. "What do you see?"

"A sheet of paper?" Jamie guessed.

"Yes!" Anyone would have thought her reply had been brilliant. "One sheet of paper, one area, one white space." He gave her the pencil. "Draw a line."

She drew a slightly unsteady horizontal line about ten centimetres long in the middle of the sheet.

"Great! Now what do you see."

"A sheet... I mean a white space... with a line in it?"

"Point to the area above the line." She did.

"Now show me the area below the line." She did. "So, the line has created areas. What Escher said was that every line is a boundary – think of it like a wall. If you build a wall, you make two sides. On paper, if you draw a line, you get two sides." Jamie looked at her line, which was a boundary.

"OK, now put your pencil back on that line and carry it on to join it back up as an enclosed shape – it doesn't have to be a circle, just anything which joins back up to the start – that's it."

They contemplated Jamie's line. "What have you drawn?"

"Well, it looks like half a star, but I wasn't trying to draw anything."

Mr Stevens disappeared to the back of the room again, rummaged around once more and came back with a pair of scissors. "Put the point of the scissors through any point on the line and cut round the shape you drew."

Jamie did and neatly put her half a star down on the table-top. She was about to bin the waste trimming when Mr Stevens stopped her. "No, keep that. How many shapes have you drawn."

"One." At last Jamie was sure of something.

"Sure?"

"Sure." Whenever a teacher asked you that, you knew you were wrong, but Jamie couldn't see whatever the trick was.

"So, what's this?" Mr Stevens held up the rest of the sheet

from which Jamie had cut out her half-star.

"Left-overs."

"But it's equally a shape, and it was created just as much by your line as the shape inside the line."

"But it just looks a mess."

Mr Stevens gave a triumphant smile. "And that was what made Escher a genius. When he drew lines, he could see the shapes he was making inside them *and* outside them, at the same time. You have a look some time at the patterns he made. Good God, is that the time – I'm supposed to be in a meeting," and he left her.

She sat there clutching a new way of thinking and two scruffy bits of paper.

Later that evening, Jamie reviewed what she'd written. She wasn't sure what Justin and Gavin would make of it, but she reckoned it would get Ryan's attention. If she could photograph the two pictures in the Head's Office, she could put copies of them in with her article.

HAVE YOU EVER WONDERED WHY THERE IS NO LIVING CREATURE WITH THREE PAIRS OF LEGS WHICH CAN CURL UP INTO A WHEEL WHEN THE GOING GETS ROUGH?

M.C. ESCHER was so annoyed by this creature of his imagination which wanted to exist — and didn't — that he drew it and worked out a 3D representation of how it would move. He drew dozens of them walking and rolling up and down stairs.

He even suggested how a male version and a female version would mate (but we won't go into that).

His creature was called 'Curl-up' or rather...

the truth is, it was translated as 'Curl-up' and he really called his creature the *Pedalternorotandomovens centroculatus articulosus*

— M C Escher, from
'the World of Black and White', 1959

'Nobody can draw a line that is not a boundary line ...
In addition, every closed contour no matter what
its shape, pure circle or whimsical splash
accidental in form, evokes the sensation
of inside and outside'

If you see stairs in any Escher drawing, try and walk up — or down — them in your imagination and you'll find you are in an impossible world.

When you think about it, we expect artists to represent the 3D world in 2D by little tricks e.g. drawing smaller trees in the background to make them seem further away

Instead, Escher uses the little tricks of perspective and Maths-art to create a totally mad world — or is it a more truly 2D world?

It's not surprising he worked mostly in black and white when he uses mirror images, symmetry, shapes and reflections so much.

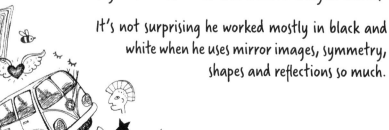

It was with some satisfaction that Jamie mailed her research on Escher to Ryan and her edited version of his emails, which she was publishing as *Myrddin in America,* and she was disappointed that nothing came back. Perhaps he was starting to settle in, make real friends instead of messing around with the men in black.

She wandered around the house, unsettled. The rugby was blaring from the living room so she passed by. She raided the biscuit tin in the kitchen, saw Chris coming into the yard, and graciously acknowledged his wave with a smile. He'd been pretty friendly since the near-disaster, almost human. He certainly looked and smelt better when he was sober.

Her thoughts drifted... why did Mr Travis want to see her? He'd probably seen *On the Other Hand* and was pleased with her enterprise. Perhaps she'd get a prize in the Awards Evening, for once, instead of not quite getting top grades, not quite being a 'most improved' and definitely not being a sports star. She returned to the biscuit tin, taking a handful of rations back to her bedroom, just in case.

Mrs Williams didn't feel like going straight to bed when she came home that night from work at Tesco so she made herself a cup of tea and switched on the television news. It was the usual depressing mixture of riots, politics and financial problems, with yet another horrific incident in a school in America.

There were photographs of sobbing students, saying how weird their classmates were in their gangster clothes and dark glasses, but that no one had taken them seriously, everyone just thought they were fantasising when they talked about shooters, no one believed they would walk into a classroom with guns and spray bullets round the room.

No-one ever thought they would kill a teacher, a classroom assistant and two classmates, leaving another teacher and five teenagers wounded, in hospital. Everyone thought these were just kids, posers, with some silly nickname. Mrs Williams had seen enough and switched off the screen. Thank God, her two weren't like that – although they had their moments. She was soon in bed, snoring safely by her husband's side.

CHAPTER 12

"Why didn't you ask me before doing this?" Mr Travis waved a copy of *The Big Issue* at Jamie. Her heart sank. It didn't look like she was up for prizes.

"You said you were too busy, Sir."

"Not so busy I couldn't say, 'This is a stupid idea – don't do it!'"

"But why is it a stupid idea, Sir? People get *The Big Issue* and they get our newsletter in it, just like in the old days when people slagged off the government in broadsheets and went to prison for it, and they find out all about being left-handed and how it ought to be equal opportunities and it isn't."

"Woah, Jamie, slow down. What you've written is good, but you should have had permission to use the computer room and all the paper."

"Sir, I did! Mr Watts said I could."

"Yes, but only because you told him it was for me."

"Well it was. I thought you'd be pleased."

"I'd be better pleased if you'd asked me. Anyway, you are definitely not to put the next edition in *The Big Issue*..."

"But I don't see what's wrong with *The Big Issue*."

"There's nothing wrong with it but it has certain... political views… and the Head would be really unhappy if the school seemed to support those views."

"But you bought that *Big Issue*, Sir, didn't you, so it must be all right. Couldn't you make the Head understand?"

"That's not the point. And no, definitely not."

Jamie had suddenly realised something more positive implied in Sir's ban on marketing via *The Big Issue*. "You said, 'next edition'."

"Yes," he responded cautiously.

"So, I can carry on?"

"That's what I've been saying, isn't it? Only I want a copy to me before you print it for the whole school, so I can check there's nothing to get you in front of the Head again."

She might have been interesting to interview, and left-handed, but Jamie really did not want to visit the Head's Office again. Those blue eyes could freeze the atmosphere enough to weld skin to metal. A horrible thought dawned. "Am I going to have to see the Head, over *The Big Issue*?"

"Not this time," Mr Travis indicated a pile of copies of *On the Other Hand*. "I relieved your friend of his remaining copies, so I don't see why it would reach the Head's attention – this time."

Jamie felt a pang of guilt. "But Keith must have thought he was in trouble, like he was being raided or something."

"Keith?"

"The man who sells *The Big Issue*."

"Indeed, Keith. Well, well. No, I don't think... Keith... was worried. I told him that we'd run out of copies in school so we'd like his back, please."

Jamie was relieved. Keith had been so willing to help her and distribute her newsletter. Why was it that you had a good idea and there was always some hidden reason why it wasn't a good idea at all? It did make you wonder why you bothered.

"Jamie?" She shrugged her curls out of her eyes and looked at the teacher. "It was very enterprising. You're going to be a millionaire one day while I'm still carrying the marking home. Just don't add to my grey hairs or bring on a heart attack while you're here?"

"Sir."

"*The Myrddin letter*? Nice touch, that. How's Ryan doing?"

"He says it's good for his writing, being somewhere different, being an outsider, but he wants to come home." Did he? She hadn't heard from him for a while now. Had he stopped being an outsider? After all, he hadn't lived in Port Talbot all his life like she had. He'd just adopted it as home.

"Well, pass on my regards, and I'll confirm with Mr Watts that you can use the computer room – just remember to show me a copy first." Jamie was dismissed.

Jamie called on her mother in work before going home.

She scuffed her shoes against the checkout counter, watching her mother deftly moving groceries from the conveyor belt to the scanner and weighing plate, then on for packing. Without pausing to think, she noticed the meat and put it into a flimsy bag before sending it along with the rest of the goods.

Right brain at work, Jamie thought. *When you can do a job without thinking about it, your right brain can do it for you and your left brain can get on with other thoughts, like holidays or winning the lottery.* It was supposed to be like that for drivers, but Jamie couldn't imagine doing all those movements with hands and pedals without having to think about each move.

When there was a lull, Jamie asked her mother, "What happens if someone's left-handed?"

"They can still do shopping, Jamie. And cleaning too, as I keep telling you."

"No, I mean someone working on a checkout here."

"I don't know, doesn't make any difference."

"Yes, it does," Jamie objected. "A left-hander would have to cross her arms to pick up the goods or use her right hand. It's all the wrong way round."

"Well they could work on the '10 items only' – there's tills facing both ways there."

"But that still discriminates on the main tills."

"I don't know, Jamie, and I really don't care. I'm not left-handed and I want better for you than working here."

"Dad says I can't go to university."

"He didn't mean it, just having a bad day. We'll find a way, love. You just work hard at school and leave us worry about the rest. Now take that bag," her mother passed some shopping over from beneath the counter, "and get off home with you. If I lose my job for gossiping with you, no one's going to get to university."

"In America," Jamie informed her mother, "a woman took a shop to court because the owner made her use her right hand at the checkout – and she won."

"I'll keep that in mind. Now take your obsession home and give me a break."

Late spring was teasing the air with a promise of summer and Jamie sat on her back doorstep, letting the breeze draw goosebumps from her arms while the sun pinked her face. There was still no word from Ryan, and it had not been the sort of evening to spend in front of a computer. She must have been softened by the sunshine because the noises coming from the coal shed sounded more melodious than usual.

At one stage, she thought she could hear a girl's voice threading through the harmony. Good for Gareth – a boy of his word. Chris put his head through the door twice, like a shy tortoise, and ducked it back in each time he saw her. The third time, his head was followed by the rest of him.

"Can I join you for a bit?" He waited for her answer, which was what decided her. If he'd sat down anyway, she'd have gone in. She'd seen too much of him thinking he could do what he liked.

"Free country," she told him. He sat beside her.

"Got a good voice, Kelly."

"Remembered her name then, have you?"

"Too scared of you not to."

"Keep it that way." There was a pause but Jamie's curiosity got the better of her. "You going out together then? You and Kelly?"

"No disrespect, but she's not really my type."

"Could have fooled me."

"Just drink, that was. Anyway, you can see Gareth's the only one who exists, in her eyes."

"Can't see it myself," Jamie cheerfully dismissed her brother. "What do you do then, at college. Sports Science, like Gareth?"

"No, A levels. English, French and History."

Jamie twisted sharply to look at him but he was too close to her on the step to catch his eye comfortably, and she turned back quickly to face the path. He didn't sound like he was joking. Perhaps it was just too hard to believe a boy had a brain at all, when you'd only heard him crooning soppy songs, or seen him tanked up.

"That's what I want to do," she confessed. "English is my favourite."

Before she quite knew how it had happened, she was telling Chris about her writing and about *On the Other Hand,* and they were both shivering in the evening air by the time he said, "I'd better go" and he did.

Her parents' bedroom door was ajar and she couldn't help noticing her father, back towards her, trying to comb his hair with his left hand while looking down at a sheet of paper on the dressing-table. She smiled, recognising the banner of her broadsheet. Perhaps there would be a right (right?!) time to tell him that no one was sure what caused left-handedness, but that there did seem to be some genetic link. If both parents were left-handed, then the odds of children being right-handers rather than left-handers were 2:1 compared with 50:1 from two right-handed parents. Perhaps she would tell him – or perhaps she would just carry on leaving copies of *On the Other Hand* around the house.

She checked before she went to bed but there was still nothing from Ryan.

LEFT-HANDER OF THE WEEK: DR ALBERT SCHWEITZER

Born in Alsace, Schweitzer was a brilliant musician as well as scientist, philosopher and missionary. He spent many years working in Africa where he had a pet cat, Sizi. Because the cat liked sleeping on his left hand while Schweitzer worked at his desk, he taught himself to write right-handed.

Typical left-hander's versatility!

STILL NOT SURE WHETHER YOU'RE LEFT-HANDED? TRY ...

THE THUMBNAIL TEST
The thumbnail is bigger and broader on the thumb on your dominant hand.

THE SIDEWAYS-ON TEST
Draw the face of a person — or dog, cat, rabbit — seen sideway on (profile).

THE SHOELACE TEST
Tie your shoelaces.

THE CUTLERY TEST

(use on someone else —

good for small child) Put a spoon in the middle of a place setting and see which hand the person uses to pick it up.

ANSWERS:

Sideways-on Test — If you drew a profile facing right, you're probably left-handed.

Shoelace Test — Left-handers usually cross the left lace on top first, then make the first loop to the right.

HANDEDNESS IN NATURE

LOUIS PASTEUR (FAMOUS FOR PASTEURISING MILK) WAS ONE OF THE FIRST SCIENTISTS TO OBSERVE THAT HANDEDNESS EXISTS IN ALL ASPECTS OF NATURE, EVEN IN ITS CHEMICAL COMPOSITION:

* DNA, the stuff of life which contains our genes, is a clockwise spiral

* most shells have clockwise spirals

* nearly all plants which grow in a spiral, grow clockwise

* most flatfish lie down on their left side, so are right-finned

today scientists talk about pairs of photons — a left-handed and right-handed particle.

NATURE'S LEFT-HANDERS

IT HAS BEEN SUGGESTED THAT:

* all polar bears are left-handed (No chance of me checking that one out)

* most parrots will pick up a cracker with their left claw

* an arctic whale's one tusk can grow to 9ft spiralling counter-clockwise

* bats fly out of a cave counterclockwise

* a lobster's larger claw is the dominant one, sometimes showing left-clawedness

* honeysuckle twines to the left

* gorillas' left arms are heavier than their right, suggesting left-handedness.

CHAPTER 13

Two weeks had flown by as Jamie found herself claimed by different groups of kids demanding her expert views on their 'test' results, or even on their parents' brain and hand tendencies; or complaining that the Torque Test didn't work. A Young Business Enterprise Group was trying, unsuccessfully, to talk the Head into letting them run guided tours at lunch-time to the Escher prints in her Office.

The IT Club had designed and were selling *Left-handed and proud of it* badges (having binned one prototype which showed a gesture that was no less rude for having been common in ancient Rome).

Jamie had stopped checking her email and had almost stopped feeling hurt, so it jolted her back into confusion when a casual scan showed that, yes, there was mail. It had to be Ryan. She was so angry at the lack of replies, of interest, of anything from him for so long, that she nearly deleted it without reading it. But she didn't.

Jamie, I'm rushing about but Ryan wanted me to let you know he's all right, in case you worried when you watched the news. He's in hospital and he'll get in touch with you when he can.

Hospital? News? All right? Jamie couldn't read on for the flood of panic. How could she have thought he couldn't be bothered any more. How could she not have known something terrible must have happened? She'd even thought of warning him about those 'friends'. Heart hammering as she thought about the kids he was mixing with, she tried to focus.

It's like breaking into Fort Knox just getting into his computer, more passwords than the FBI. He's such a secretive person and I don't know what-all he's thinking especially now this has happened. I don't want to pry and we all need our space but I just happened across files on here with Myrddin as signatory. Can you help me out here? Is this some friend of his?

Of course, we've had the Atlanta PD round but they talked to Ryan without me there, and I just have this feeling he's keeping something back to do with this Myrddin. The police took the computer away and I don't know why or what they found on it. Maybe the answer is in the Myrddin files? There's so much on here I don't know where to start looking.

Hope you all are fine. You take care, you hear. Catch you again.

Atlanta PD – what was that. PD? She remembered LA PD on television. Police Department! It just got worse. She'd known something awful was going to happen and it had. But what? All Jamie had were questions and a week gone by without her doing anything. She suddenly felt sick and hungry and kicked in the stomach, all at the same time, and she had to do something, anything. She knocked off a quick reply.

Please, Mrs Anderson, tell me what's going on. Why is Ryan in hospital? What's happened? I haven't seen any news and I don't know anything.

Don't worry about Myrddin. Should she tell? Ryan would kill her. But what if the police were looking for some Myrddin and missing out on what they should be doing. What if Ryan's Mum was like Jamie, worried sick? She couldn't take the risk. If Ryan were well enough to kill her, she'd cope with that.

Ryan uses Myrddin as a pen name to write articles for our magazine in school. He really doesn't want you to know so please don't let on I told you. Computer files are private – like someone's diary – Ryan wouldn't like you to go through them. Sorry if you think that's

cheeky of me but I just want you to know.

Jamie

She waited barely a minute before checking to see if there was a reply, knowing she was being foolish, not able to help it. Perhaps Ryan's Mum was online at this very moment. The empty screen stared back at her. It was more likely that Ryan's Mum was busy reading his files, his emails.

Jamie felt her face grow hot at the thought of Ryan's mother reading their emails, looking through Ryan's private writing, the poems and stories he'd started. She'd kept a diary, the year before, and Gareth had stolen it, dancing round the house, threatening to read bits aloud, and it had been her calm, unflappable mother who had flared up, slapped the top of his head and demanded the diary back.

He had been so shocked, he just handed over the little book and her mother had closed it without looking, given it to Jamie and said, "Trust goes two ways in this house. I trust you to behave right and you can trust me to leave your private things stay private. And that goes for you too, Gareth, or if you want me to search under your bed, I will." Her brother had gone crimson, but whatever had been under his bed had been moved; Jamie had been annoyed with him enough to check it out but found nothing.

She went looking for her mother now, and found her ironing and singing along to the radio. Jamie poured out the news from America, or rather the lack of it, and asked, "Has there been anything on the news?"

"No, nothing. You're probably worrying too much. It's probably a weather thing – they're always having earthquakes and tornadoes over there, aren't they. I expect he came off his bike in a gale and broke an arm or something."

"He doesn't have a bike."

"Or someone biked into him, you know what I mean. It's the general idea that counts."

"If you ask me, it's the broken arm that counts. Anyway," Jamie fretted, "that wouldn't explain the police checking his computer."

"Probably a coincidence. They might have been doing a check on some local person – there are some very nasty people about – and checking whether Ryan had talked to him, you know that chat they do on the computer."

"An online chat room."

Her mother's eyes narrowed. "You haven't been talking to strangers, have you, on the computer, I mean?"

"No, Mum." Talking to Keith certainly hadn't been online so she didn't even need to keep her fingers crossed. Trust between her and her Mum was all very well, but it had to be flexible. "It's just that Ryan was mixing with some weirdos

– no, not pervs and not online – real ones, in his class at school. He called them 'the men in black', and they wanted information from him, sick stuff."

Her mother laid out the cuff on a shirt sleeve so she could iron inside it. "I'm sure Ryan has more sense than to get involved with people like that. He always struck me as a nice boy."

"That's just it; he had this stupid plan to get in with a bad crowd and shock his mother into coming back here. He reckoned his mother would take one look at these men in black – they wore these long coats and shades and thought they were gangsters–" Jamie didn't like the way her mother had put the iron down on its heel and was staring at her.

"What is it?"

"Nothing." Her mother put the ironed shirt on its hanger and spread another one on the board. "I was just thinking. Anyway, you know Ryan's all right because his mother said so. Stop worrying. You going to do some ironing while you're here?"

"Got schoolwork to do." Jamie backed quickly out of the kitchen and went back to her bedroom, chewing the skin down the side of her fingernails. However often she checked, there were no more emails.

The next day, Mrs Williams made an appointment that enabled her to spend her lunch break in a Headteacher's office, where she took no interest in two pictures by Escher. A phone call confirmed both her worst fears and her best hopes. That only left the question of what to tell Jamie. Everything, was the answer. She was that sort of mother.

When she came home from work, Mrs Williams found her daughter in front of the computer in her son's room. "Jamie," she said softly and gently put her hands on the drooping shoulders in front of her, facing the screen. "I know what happened to Ryan. I saw the news, a couple of weeks ago, and there was an incident at an American High School where a gang of teenagers, misfits, took guns into school and used them. There were people killed and people wounded."

There was a stillness about the figure in front of her which seemed smaller and younger than usual. "You know what the news is like; it's all bombs and bodies, and I didn't think about it at all until you mentioned those boys Ryan knew, and the way you described them just reminded me of something in the news report. It still seemed too crazy to be true, and I didn't want to worry you, so I went up the school today – it was your Dad's idea – and told your Headmistress.

I asked her if she had a phone number for Ryan's Mum.

She didn't, and she said she couldn't have given it to me anyway, but she did have a number for his new school, and she called them right there in front of me. She spoke to the Principal and he told her that, yes, it was his school – you could tell from her voice how cut up he was – and he told her that there were four students in hospital with gunshot wounds, but Ryan was already in hospital before the shooting. He had appendicitis, was rushed into hospital from school, all very dramatic.

The Principal said his classmates had worried about him coming so close to his appendix bursting, and he could have died... and then the day after, it was his class..."

"And some of them did. Die," Jamie finished off for her mother, her voice shaking too. "I know. I've heard from Ryan." Tears blurring her eyes, she invited her mother to read the screen.

Hey girl, it's me. I still get tired but they finally let me come home from hospital. You have to pay for all your medical care here, and I guess Mum wanted value for money. I had real pains in the belly all day in school and they rushed me into hospital – ambulance, the works. Turns out it was appendicitis and not very clever – near to bursting – so they took my appendix out and kept me in. Meanwhile,

I guess you know by now, the men in black completely flipped, took guns into school and — I still don't believe this is true — killed people.

I'm getting loads of visitors from my class, never been so popular, but it's you I need to talk to. They're coming to be kind, sure, but they're also coming because they need to tell me about it. Because I'm the one who wasn't there, I'm the one they can tell. After the first two were crying and saying how it was for them, I felt I had to write about it so the world knows how it was and how it is. Then everyone was coming to see me and my notebook was full and I've written it up for you and for them. Don't let me down, Jamie, publish it for me, so they know in Afan what it was like, so people spot the signs and it doesn't happen again.

I feel so guilty that I was safe all the time, and so dirty that I knew them, that perhaps I could have stopped them, and the worst feeling of all is wanting to hide from being so scared, knowing I'd have hidden behind any piece of furniture, any human being if I'd been in that classroom because when they came in, they asked for me.

I'm never going to know whether they still thought I was 'their man' or whether they were planning to 'waste' me first. I have nightmares, Jamie, such nightmares. Can you imagine what it was like for those who were there?

It's not how I planned it but I'm coming home. My Mum's jittery after all this and doesn't feel safe any more. I guess that part of my plan has worked but now I know what that's like, I don't think it was such a clever idea. I hate seeing her scared to open a door or walk down the street after dark. I guess she'll be back to normal in time.

She's found out about me being a writer because all these kids calling told her what I was doing, so I came clean and told her about Myrddin's published articles in the past. I even showed her our magazine, the campaign, everything, and she was real quiet (for once!) and I guess the big hug and kiss meant she was pleased.

She didn't really seem surprised, like she thought it was in the genes or something (maybe she knows an extra something about that sperm donor but she's not letting on!) Makes a change though for her just to accept something. Thing is, I want to be accepted for myself and I was worried that she would look at my writing and say, "That's wonderful," if she was in a good mood or "That's crap," if she was in a bad mood and I'd still have no way of knowing if I was any good. You and me have delivered the goods, without someone on our back.

About our campaign, I've been thinking a lot these last weeks and I think I've got the answers to two of our questions about life. I hate labels – like Mrs Davies' favourites – gender, race, disability – and I think equality is a state of mind. The second answer? You'll have to wait for that till I see you. Won't be long.

Ryan.

CHAPTER 14

'MY CLASSMATES SHOT MY TEACHER AND MY FRIENDS'

On 15th June at 2.37pm, I was rushed into hospital with severe appendicitis; on 16th June at 11.46am, four fellow-students brought guns into the school and turned them on my class. If I had not been in hospital, I might have been fatally shot, instead of Cassie, Joel, Mrs McManus or Mr Montgomery; I might have been shot and wounded instead of Danny, Winona, Duffy, Benjamin or Raphael.

But I'm not the only one who feels like this; everyone in my class who was there is thinking "It could have been me," and feeling glad and guilty that it wasn't. We need to know what happened. We need to know what went wrong. We need to try to stop it happening again, so we can try to do what is right by our dead classmates.

Micky told me what it was like for him. "There was a kind of stir at the back of the room. The door was still swinging from them walking in. It's as if your brain goes slow and I was just thinking, 'Hey the men in black are way late – are they going to be in trouble with Mr Montgomery and, boy, has he got a sharp tongue,' and even when I was thinking all this I was watching their coats swing open and Mr Montgomery going down and then other kids. You couldn't tell who had been hit and who was diving for cover. And I just stood there like a fool and I still don't know how I'm here. Don't get the wrong idea – I wasn't brave – I was like a rabbit in a car head-lights – I just froze."

Marnie's memories are of shutting her eyes; "I just kept saying, over and over again, this is not happening. The noise of the gunshots was earbursting, and when it stopped I thought I was deaf and I was afraid to open my eyes in case it was still going on and I couldn't hear it. It seemed like for hours and then, when I opened my eyes, there was red on my arm, blood, and I just rubbed and rubbed, and then I realised it wasn't mine, it was Cassie's. I've never seen a dead body before. I have bad dreams and the doctor's given me something to help."

Jake told me that what he would never forget was one of the 'men in black' Luther looking down at Joel. "He took off the dark glasses and you could see he knew what they had done and it wasn't like he'd thought it would be, it wasn't like Ricky had told him it would be. He was only Ricky's little brother doing what his big brother said and you could see him thinking, "Oh God, what have I done?" He wasn't in our class, he was only ninth grade. His coat was way too big for him."

All the witnesses agreed that there had been no planning for what they would do after the killing; the men in black just stood round holding their guns loosely "like handbags" one girl said. "Ricky kicked Mr Montgomery's body and came out with some tough comment about paying him back but you could tell that his heart wasn't in it and that he was sick scared."

Many students said that they didn't believe that the other killings had been planned. "It just seemed to happen with guns going off and bullets spraying. There was no reason for those students to be the ones who got hit. The shooters were a group who kept to themselves, weird, and no one hung out with them except you, the new boy from England. They asked for you, but you'd been taken to hospital the day before, with appendicitis."

So now you know. I was mixing with four boys who were nicknamed 'the men in black' – I think they nicknamed themselves and it stuck – and who posed as gangsters, wearing black (of course) long coats, even in summer, dark glasses, walking and talking tough. I didn't like them and I was using them to annoy my mother with my 'bad company'. They treated me like a mascot, the 'brains' of their gang, able to use a computer to find out everything they wanted to know.

The police interviewed me. When they saw the websites and material I had downloaded, on weapons, bombs, and killing, the interviews grew harder. They told me I was either very clever and evil, or very stupid. After hours of interviews, they concluded I was stupid, and I got off with a warning.

The internet is no different from the real world. If it's illegal to get or spread some information in the real world, then it's just as illegal on the internet. The difference is that it's easy to get on the internet, and you can break the law by accident by clicking on a dodgy site. In the eyes of the law, it's the same as buying drugs from a dealer. It's your responsibility to stay clean, away from drugs, porn, terrorist information and illegal photographs.

I knew what I was doing wasn't good but I didn't know I was breaking the law. I knew to ask myself whether information on the internet was true. I knew lots of ways of checking whether it was true; I never asked whether it was good.

I will never know whether the information and

pictures I gave to those boys, when I knew they were disturbed people, helped them kill my teacher and my classmates. I don't know why it was Mr Montgomery they chose. Ricky was always bearing grudges against teachers for the smallest remarks, and the others had this idea that their careers would be in organised crime, like you see in films.

They guarded the toilets, they ran a protection racket to get money from other kids, they played with the roles that would make them seem big – and then they played with guns. No-one who was in that classroom wants to see a gun again.

That is the last time I will call them the men in black or any other nickname. The label being used for them now is 'killers'. They are Ricky, his little brother Luther, Scott and Harvey Junior. They are all under sixteen and they are on trial for murder.

Myrddin, Atlanta High School, Georgia

Jamie buried her face in her mother's arms. "What can I say to him?" she murmured.

"He's your friend. Whatever you say will be the right thing."

It was not as easy as that, either by email or during those first meetings when Ryan and his mother returned to the house up the hill from Jamie in Port Talbot. Everyone was careful with each other, working out how much could be said.

Gradually, the laughter was coming back, from comments like Jamie's instinctive, "You've gone so pale!" and Ryan's ironic, "Not near so pale as you girl. I'm used to seeing sunshine skins around me now, you know."

He would laugh but, then, the shadows would be back, perhaps the memories of those who would not laugh again. It was near the end of term so he had not started school again yet, but his *Myrddin letters from America* had added to his reputation around the school and those kids who saw him around mostly showed respect.

There were of course, the odd ones who rushed up to him and asked, "Was there loads of blood?" but he was man enough to shrug them off easily by saying, "I wasn't there." He had always been man enough, Jamie thought, aching for him.

"Meet me after school tomorrow, in the hall," she told him, one evening when the setting sun gilded the glass on the shopping centre and sent shadows up the river towards the green gorges of the Afan Valley. "I've got a surprise for you."

"Once I'm in, they'll keep me there."

"Naaa, not you, not with just a week to go till the holidays."

Jamie was already sitting in the hall when Ryan announced his arrival with a hand on her shoulder. She couldn't hear him for the noise of the amplified music, and they had to speak directly into each other's ears.

"Rehearsal," she explained unnecessarily, "for the end of term disco. They auditioned, and I think the clincher was Gareth being an ex-pupil. Don't tell him that though – he thinks he's God's gift to music."

They watched her brother leading his band in some synchronised jumps, belting out some lyrics, sharing the verses with Chris and Rob. Then they all came in on the chorus. Someone missed a step, they all lost it, and Gareth switched the music off to shout at the others and reorganise.

They sorted themselves out and then, unexpectedly, Chris came to the front and introduced a new song, "one I've written for a special girl who hits hard and looks gorgeous." Jamie's cheeks burned as he launched into the lyrics.

"Everyone's a fool on times
Tries to be cool on times
reaches dark places
with no friendly faces
but luck in the night
will bring you the sight
someone like Jamie
she's the one who saved me
she's the one..."

Jamie couldn't move without drawing attention to herself nor did it help to sit still. She just had to listen for three minutes, while Chris focused all his attention on his audience: her and Ryan. It was a relief when the band performed a dance routine in the middle of the song, but back came the lyrics, well sung, she had to admit, but unrelenting.

"This what you wanted me here for?" Ryan asked wickedly.

"Didn't know he'd done that. Just words," she mumbled, still red-faced, glad that the band was already organising itself, with Gareth up front again for their next number.

In the lull, Jamie asked the question which had been on her mind for over a month.

"You said you had the answer to the second question."

Like her, Ryan was looking straight ahead at the band

bickering, "No, not that way, not this way!" She could feel him hesitate before responding.

"You asked me about me feeling more at home where I wasn't the only black kid. Truth is, I've moved around so much, I never fit in, never feel at home. Mostly I don't mind – it's interesting. But one time, I felt it, felt at home, found those roots, all of that." Jamie waited. "When I came here and you didn't worry about who I was, or what I was like, you just said, "Did you know the Queen has to have toilets built specially when she visits some place."

"Well she does!" Jamie defended herself. "Anyway, I was younger then."

"We both were. But I came back, didn't I."

"Look," Jamie said, "that's what I wanted you to see." A slight figure, who'd been at the side of the stage, turned into Kelly, and walked up front to take her place beside Gareth, as if she belonged there. Someone started the backing track, and the two singers moved into a duet, dancing as they sang, playing off each other's moves.

The rest of the band acted as backing singers with some melodic 'shoobies', and it gave Jamie – and presumable Kelly – great satisfaction to see Chris staying well in the background, giving her the limelight.

"She's all right," commented Ryan.

"She is, isn't she." Jamie felt as proud of Kelly as if she

promoted her, which in a way she had.

"Not my kind of music but she's got the voice."

"And the moves," Ryan said, as Kelly flicked her skirt around.

Jamie made a non-committal noise.

"I've got a surprise for you too," he told her. "Your house, after school tomorrow night."

Jamie wasn't sure she wanted any more surprises, but she didn't have any option. When she saw the cardboard box Ryan was carrying, she wasn't sure whether to be less, or more, apprehensive. The minute she heard the contents, she knew what the surprise was.

She didn't open the box. It didn't do to give your heart where it could only get hurt. "Ry, what if I can't keep it?" she asked him, round-eyed.

"This is the new responsible me. My Mum helped me choose her, and she checked with your Mum, and *she* said your Dad was all for it, so they aren't a problem. Are you going to open it or what?"

Jamie let the kitten out of the box. Its eyes were just turning from blue to green and it hissed and spat at the strange surroundings, and then purred as Jamie stroked it.

"Just like Kelly."

Jamie laughed. "Wait here; don't let it get into trouble." She reappeared with a cotton reel dangling on a string. She held it high enough for the kitten to bat with its paw but not too high for it to reach.

"See!" she declared triumphantly.

"What? She's playful."

"No, stupid. She's left-pawed, look." Sure enough, the kitten was leading with its left, each time it attacked the bobbling cotton reel.

"What shall we call her?"

"What do you think?"

ACKNOWLEDGEMENTS

With thanks to:

the Ballyvourney Library Teen Book Club for their invaluable help with the 13th Sign edition: Art, Caitriona Donncha, Liam, Maebh and, of course, Kristin; all those lefties; to all those (too many to name) who run websites about left-handers; to Yale Librarians for their help with Benjamin Franklin's archives; and to Martin for his invaluable pre-editing suggestions.

Right Hand, Left Hand, Chris McManus
The Left-Hander's Handbook, James T. de Kay
The Left-Hander's Guide to Life, Leigh W Rutledge and Richard Donley
The Magic of M C Escher, designed by Erik Thé

Resources for teachers are free to download, use and adapt, from *www.jeangill.com*

THE STORY OF JAMIE AND RYAN CONTINUES IN FORTUNE KOOKIE

Can dreams take over your life?

Jamie's mother is hooked on fortune-tellers, and running the family into debt. To cure her, Jamie decides to investigate the psychic world, and to show that it is a rip-off, with the help of her best friend, Ryan.

Their research causes havoc in school and they are drawn deeper into the very world they are investigating. Jamie's dreams of walking a medieval battlefield are so vivid that she feels compelled to resolve a historical mystery that starts at Kidwelly Castle in South Wales, where Princess Gwenllian once lived.

Caught up in what seem to be supernatural events, Jamie doesn't know what to believe and is sleepwalking into danger. Will friendship be strong enough to bring her back into the real world?

IF YOU LIKED MY BOOK, PLEASE HELP OTHER READERS FIND IT BY WRITING A REVIEW.

THANK YOU.

You can contact me at *jeangill.com*

I love to hear from readers.

For exclusive offers and news of my books sign up at my website for my newsletter.

You can follow me on twitter: *@writerjeangill*

Find me on facebook: *facebook.com/writerjeangill/*

ABOUT THE AUTHOR

I'm a Welsh writer and photographer living in the south of France with scruffy dogs, a Nikon D750 and a man. I taught English in Wales for many years and my claim to fame is that I was the first woman to be a secondary headteacher in Carmarthenshire. I'm mother or stepmother to five children so life has been pretty hectic.

I've published all kinds of books, both with conventional publishers and self-published. You'll find everything under my name from prize-winning poetry and novels, military history, translated books on dog training, to a cookery book on goat cheese. My work with top dog-trainer Michel Hasbrouck has taken me deep into the world of dogs with problems, and inspired one of my novels.

With Scottish parents, an English birthplace and French residence, I can usually support the winning team on most sporting occasions.

AUTHOR INTERVIEW

Are you left-handed?
No, I'm very right-handed.

What gave you the idea for the book?
A lot of different thoughts suddenly came together. My husband, one stepdaughter and a close friend are all left-handed and it has fascinated me for some time to watch how they do things. When my friend Lesley and I were going fishing, she would drive and as she is totally confused about left and right, I had to say 'turn your way' or 'turn my way' to give directions. My husband, on the other hand (!) says he never confused left and right until I wrote a book on the subject, and he is very good with his hands – I'm the clumsy one. Then, in addition to personal contacts, I was training teachers about literacy, and I realised that other trainers didn't often consider left-handers. The final spark was a book another friend lent to me, 'Drawing on the right side of the brain', all about the different jobs done by the two halves of the brain.

All of a sudden, I could see these imaginary characters, Jamie and Ryan, finding out some of this stuff, and I wanted them and their story to be influenced by what they find out, so that the facts aren't just stuck into the novel, they're part of it.

How did you do the research?

I asked any left-handed people that I knew, a lot of questions, such as what it had been like in school or what annoyed them. I read any books I could find on the subject and I looked up lots of websites.

Did you find out anything that surprised you?

When I started asking groups of teachers whether they were left- or right-handed, I couldn't believe how few of them are left-handed, a lot fewer than 1 in 10, which is the ratio in the general population. This seems stranger to me than the high proportion of left-handed tennis players or artists and I don't know of any scientifically sound research into these oddities. Many of the facts that Jamie and Ryan find out surprised me and I hadn't realised how handedness works in nature, in spirals for instance. I certainly hadn't appreciated how people had been persecuted – in the past I hope – for being left-handed. The biggest surprise was how all my left-handers in real life just accept a right-hand world and get on with making the most of it.

Do you have a favourite character?

I spent the most time with Jamie and Ryan so I know most about them and care very much what happens to them. I suppose I see myself as more like Ryan than like Jamie in that I was a soldier's daughter, so I always had to move house as a child and was always the outsider. I really identify with Ryan being told not to leave marks on a house that's not really theirs. I was never as cool as Ryan though – more like Jamie in lacking confidence. But I can't say I have a favourite character – I have a soft spot for Kelly because she has talent and guts; for the Head of English who's getting nagged at home for working too hard; and most of all for Keith, *The Big Issue* seller. When he says 'Bad that', it's my favourite line in the whole book. There have been so many times in my life I would just have liked someone to say 'Bad that.'

How do you know the facts in the book are true?

I don't. And one of the difficulties with the research was that there is a lot published which definitely isn't true – websites saying someone famous is left-handed and then that person stating that he's not. I tried to cross-check facts by using different sources and I left out a lot of assertions that are founded on dubious statistics or are misleading in their conclusions.

Suppose someone does a survey that finds out that people with bigger feet do better in exams and the survey concludes that having big feet is a sign of intelligence; what's wrong with this is that they don't mention that the people with bigger feet are 16 years old and the people with smaller feet are 10, so in fact it is growing up that is the cause of the greater intelligence not the feet size. This is a really important difference, between cause and correlation.

With regard to left-handers, a 'fact' often quoted is that left-handers die younger than right-handers and the conclusion is that they are killed by their clumsiness in a right-handed world. The actual fact is that there are fewer left-handers among the oldest people in the population than in the population as a whole. This might well be because when they were young, parents and schools often forced left-handers to write right-handed. You have to be very careful with interpreting statistics – and that's if the statistics are reliable in the first place.

Where do you write?
My desk looks out of the window onto the garden and I write there, on my laptop, but I write poems anywhere, on anything – backs of chequebooks, shopping lists – and I always write poetry by hand first.

How do you plan your books?
Carefully. I usually have a rough outline of the plot so that I know what will be in a chapter, but I do change details or twists in the narrative as I write. I didn't like writing an autobiographical account of a year in France because I didn't know what was going to happen next.

Was there one bit that was harder to write than the rest?
Yes, the tragic incident was very difficult to write. I don't like people getting their kicks from watching all the most horrible news that they can find and saying 'how awful'

and it worried me that I was doing the same sort of thing, enjoying how awful something was. What helped me write it was the idea that writing was a way of thinking about what happened and why, with the idea that if we know why, we can prevent these sorts of things. Not saying 'how awful' about the whole world but looking at just one bad thing beside us, eyes open, and saying 'Well? What are we going to do about it?'

Which part is your favourite?

I like the ending, I like moments between Ryan and Jamie, just in the way they talk to each other, when I think their friendship is something very special. The bit that was the most fun to write was where the boys from the band get tanked up in the coal shed but it could have had such dangerous consequences.

Do you care what people think about what you write?

Very much. I don't feel that what I've written has come alive until someone reads it and enjoys it. I am very interested in a reader telling me what he or she liked about something I've written. I can and do accept constructive criticism before something is published but it's not much use to me afterwards, and nobody enjoys being criticised. If you listen to enough criticism, you'll get total contradictions, which just shows you how subjective it all is. For instance, one professional critic thought that the book was too politically correct; another thought it was unacceptable because it was 'anti-American'.

Do you think it is anti-American?

Good question. Ryan is anti-American because he's been forced to move there, leaving his best friend, and he doesn't see himself as American, even though his mother wants him to; in so far as we see America through Ryan's eyes, then yes, it is anti-American, but it also gives a lot of detail on American life – and American left-handers – and you might notice that Ryan is starting to use American expressions, the longer he lives there. As for the 'tragic incident', it is a fact that more of those sorts of incidents occur in America, but it could and does happen in Europe too.

On balance, no, I don't think it is anti-American but, suppose it was, so what? If it's pro-Welsh, so what? Don't I have the right to show the world as I see it? And you, as a reader, to make your own mind up?

Do you see yourself as a Welsh writer?

Yes. I'm proud of being a member of the Welsh Academi and much of what I write was born in Wales, even if I wasn't, even if I'm not actually writing about Wales. I lived and worked in Wales for 25 years and that will always be part of me. I have lived in France for 18months now in dazzling sunny weather, amongst mountains, lavender and olive trees, and I love it; but I love Wales too. The French say that I'm 'Welsh Provençal' and I' am happy with that, although my Scottish parents wouldn't have been.

What are you going to write next?

I'm in the middle of writing a cookery book because I love cheese and live in the middle of a fantastic goat cheese region in France. I also have several ideas for the next novel and I don't know which to choose first – once I start it will take me about a year to write it and I won't be able to do anything else, so choosing is important.

BOOK 2 SAMPLE OF THE SERIES
LOOKING FOR NORMAL: FORTUNE KOOKIE

CHAPTER 1

"You're not serious?" Ryan grabbed his friend's arm so he could stop her walking and check her expression but there was no hint of fun in the clear blue of her eyes. "No one's mother could be that stupid, especially yours."

Jamie shook her head. "At first I thought she was doing it for a laugh, but she was on the phone for hours so I had a look at the bill. She keeps all that stuff so tidy in a drawer and Dad never goes there. And it was all there, sometimes every day she's calling, and not just this month, neither."

"So, what are we going to do about it?" Ryan's whole face wrinkled up as he considered the problem and he missed the grateful look that came his way.

"I have this idea," she admitted, "but I need help."

"That's enough gossip, you two – you're late," Mr Jones pointed out, tapping his watch as he ushered the tail end of a queue into the Science Lab.

"Why do they do that?" muttered Ryan, "as if we're foreigners who need pictures to go with the words or something."

"It's in their training," replied Jamie under her breath, as Ryan flashed his teeth widely at Mr Jones.

"Sorry Sir," he said, "we were checking the weather station and we got into discussion over whether there was any connection between climate change and the planet's magnetic fields."

The teacher's eyes lit up with the inner glow of too-rarely indulged obsession. "Funny you should say that," he began, waving vaguely at the rest of the class to sit down, and frowning at three restless characters doomed to the front bench for previous misbehaviours. "There is a very exciting documentary coming up on TV…"

Jamie let the teacher-speak wash over her. She was used to this situation from hanging around with Ryan, and the important thing was that she'd managed to talk to him, and that something was going to happen. That, too, was not unusual with Ryan.

For the tenth time, Ryan said, "I just can't believe it. Now if it was my mother–" he broke off and they listened to Mrs Anderson bashing away on a laptop, occasionally coming out with a "Goddam" or, more obscurely, "bill of rights mean nothing to you guys?"

Ryan's mother was a journalist who still kept her American links although she lived in Wales now. She'd lived there long enough to stop calling it Wales, England" but she still found ways to embarrass her son.

To give his mother her due, as Ryan often said, she would have been an embarrassment anywhere. He could not understand that Jamie was a little in awe of Mrs Anderson's glamour, her southern States accent and the way she talked about her book on the federal states of Europe, as if writing such a thing was normal parent behaviour – as if writing anything was normal.

Knowing, as Jamie did, that Jamie's mother had "got Ryan from a sperm bank" as he had told his friend when they first shared confidences, did not make Mrs Ryan any less awesome.

Moreover, for all Ryan's complaints – that his mother's attention was the sort of brilliant light best suited to torturing people in war films, and that she was just "too much" – it was Jamie's Mum who was the problem.

"Tell me the facts again." Ryan had rigged up his bedroom as Operation Headquarters. An old basketball poster (one of his Mom's doomed attempts to keep him in touch with his American roots) had been blu-tacked, face to the wall, for use as a memo-board, and Ryan was poised in front of it with a marker.

"She's phoning horoscopes for hours every week and it's costing hundreds of pounds."

Ryan wrote 'horoscopes' 'phone' and '££££' randomly in capital letters on the poster. "Start at the beginning," he prompted.

Jamie thought. "I suppose she used to check her horoscope in the paper, watch those people on daytime telly – you know, reading the stars and so on. When she wasn't working, and Dad wasn't around–"

Ryan wrote 'TV'and 'paper' in lower case letter beside 'PHONE', and drew a circle round them, then found another space for 'DAD'.

Jamie had been lying on the carpet, but sat up when she saw his addition.

"Cross that out," she said, "that's got nothing to do with it. If he's there, she can't watch stuff like that on telly because he has his programmes on, that's all. It's not like she's waiting to get rid of him so she can do stuff, more like–" Ryan raised an eyebrow. "–more like, she does different stuff when he's not there," she tailed off.

"We put it all up, then we decide what's relevant," Ryan decreed, "not before."

"But you make it look like she's having an affair or something."

"Is she?" Ryan asked, with interest.

"No!"

"How do you know?"

"I just do."

Ryan turned towards his poster, marker hovering and Jamie said, "Don't you dare."

He sighed and left it, or at least wrote nothing. "So, your Dad knows your Mum spends hours – and loads of money – on fortune tellers."

"No," Jamie admitted. "I'm sure he doesn't know because I'd have heard the roof flying off the house if he found out. He'd go nuclear."

"So how come he doesn't know?" Ryan didn't let Jamie to answer. "Either he's really thick, and notices nothing, or she's being clever at hiding things…" Ryan suddenly registered Jamie's reaction. "Sorry Jamie, I'm just being objective, I don't mean–"

"That my Dad's a moron and my Mum's a liar?"

"That's not what I said."

"You might as well have. I don't know why I bothered telling you." Jamie pulled herself up and headed for the door, shaking off Ryan's attempt to hold her back.

"Wait. I've got an idea. Look at this."

Jamie hesitated, her cheeks still flaming with angry colour, while Ryan turned back to the poster and drew an arrow from 'paper' to 'telly' to 'phone'.

"It's getting worse, isn't it?" he stabbed the poster. "She's checking it more often, and she wants direct contact with the fortune teller now – and it's costing more, isn't it? The phone bills are getting more expensive. Am I right?"

Jamie slowly closed the door handle, nodding reluctantly. "Yes. It's getting to be every day sometimes, if she thinks no one will notice. And I know we haven't got the money, Ry, so I don't know how she's paying."

"So, she's hiding things – not by lying," he added hastily, "just by doing things so as other people won't know."

Jamie shrugged. "She does all the money stuff so Dad wouldn't know about that. And I sometimes hear bits of the phone calls but with her and Dad on shifts, they're never home together, or Dad's down the pub, so he wouldn't hear, and Gareth's always out or in the coal shed practising with the band."

"So, what have you heard on the phone."

"Not a lot. It's mostly her listening for ages, then she asks a question like, "What should I do about this problem in work?" and she'll say what the problem is – it's always really boring, like a security guard trying to get extra discount or something like that.

Or she'll say she's thinking of making some changes round the house, is this a good time? I thought she was talking to a friend at first, but then I heard her saying, "Thank you

Madam Sosotris," or some name like that, and then I kept hearing odd words like 'Capricorn', and I suddenly knew what was going on.

And I knew people would just laugh about it if I said anything, because it's just normal, isn't it, reading your horoscopes and that."

"Not if you start believing in them."

"So, why do you read them?"

"I don't. But you have been known to read them aloud to me."

There was a silence. "Do you think there's anything in it, Ry?"

"No way." Less certainly, "No, no way."

"But there's loads of people check on their stars before they do things, even world leaders."

"Like who?"

"I don't know off the top my head, do I!"

Ryan grinned. "So, we find out. Step 1, know your enemy. And Mr Travis is looking for stuff for the school newletter, so we write it up and publish it."

"Oh no," Jamie groaned. "Mr Travis is *always* looking for stuff for the school newsletter."

"So, we help ourselves *and* we help him. We prove that horoscopes are rubbish, that fortune tellers are con-artists and we help your Mum. And I didn't laugh at you," he pointed out.

He turned again to his poster and stabbed at the progression from paper to phone. "And it's going to get worse again. What do you think will be the next step up after all these phone calls?"

Alone again later, Jamie reminded herself, "Horoscopes are rubbish and fortune tellers are con-artists." She looked at the search on her computer screen and started work, ignoring the nagging voice in her head, "And what if they're not?"

18458599R00110

Printed in Poland
by Amazon Fulfillment
Poland Sp. z o.o., Wrocław